WHEN THE LIGHT RETURNS...

THE DARK WAR SAGA BOOK 1

By Michael D. Nadeau

All the stories within When the Light Returns...are works of fiction. Names, characters, places, and incidents are the product of the author's imagination or used fictitiously. Any resemblance to actual persons or faeries—living, dead, or brought back to life with magical artifacts—events, or locales is coincidental. Actions, thoughts, and statements by characters do not express the desires of the author.

When the Light Returns...

First paperback edition June 2025 Michael D. Nadeau

Cover art by Daniel Eskridge- shutter stock
Typography and Interior Design by Michael D. Nadeau
Editing by Curtis Alan Provance

ISBN (paperback) 978-1-960654-04-5
ISBN (E-book) 978-1-960654-05-2

Also from
Michael D. Nadeau

The Land of Lythinall Series

The Darkness Returns
The Darkness Within
Tales From Lythinall
The Darkness Falls
The Curse of Seltemver: Tales from Lythinall: Book 2

Rise of the Archmage Series

Dragon Caller
Dragon Master

Angels Among Us

ACKNOWLEDGMENTS

I would like to thank my wife and friends for inspiring me in my writing, as well as our games that have given this tale life. Thank you to Curtis as well for editing and Alan P. for proofing.

MAP OF ALIAN'TIR

CONTENTS

CHAPTER ONE — THE DARK COMES

Castle Wrath, Isle of Raer'drin.

The light sound of bare feet on stone echoed down the corridor as he walked to his workroom in the early morning darkness. His mood was as foul as it could get, and it was no surprise that everyone was hiding in their rooms right now; everyone knew he meant business. They knew this from his attire at this very early hour: ceremonial black silk robes with gold embroidery. These robes were a sign of his station and were usually only worn for two reasons: executions and announcements, neither of which boded well for most people on the island. His warding spells had alerted him to someone tampering with his spirit warriors in his private workroom...and he had a *very* good idea who it was.

Archmage Raer'dreth Iliad, of the Great House Iliad, was a dark elf—the first, actually. Centuries ago, he had bargained with Shar'in—Goddess of Death and Shadows—for the power of shadow magic so he could command the spirits of the dead. What the archmage had *not* anticipated was the magic turning his beautiful pale skin into a deep charcoal black. It was a small price to pay for the power it gave him. Still, that power wasn't enough to hold out against the other archmages when they turned on him after the war was over.

Raer'dreth almost had it all—back during the Wasting War—but his methods frightened the elves who used to call him one of their own. He had raised the dead to fight the humans and called upon dark storms of ruin to smite their knights. When it was over, the elven archmages turned their spells on him, calling him a monster and telling him it was for his own good. They couldn't see that he was right to decimate the enemy, no matter the cost. In the end, they chose their morals, bound his powers with their combined might, and sent him to this northern, desolate island. Here, he found a barbaric people who worshiped him as a fallen god. In time, he broke the elven bindings and ushered in a new era for these people. Raer'dreth had risen out of the ashes and built himself an empire of followers that listened to his every word. After centuries of planning and hard work, the time for vengeance was at hand.

It's been a long couple of centuries since my defeat, but that is about to change, He thought as he tucked his long white hair behind his pointed ears and out of his grey eyes and walked on. *The spirits of my warriors have been with me all this time, and soon my vengeance will be released upon the lands that spurned me.* The archmage turned a corner and saw several servants scramble to get out of the way; one was sobbing as she tripped and fell in her haste. The archmage sent a shard of pure darkness at the girl, spearing her heart and silencing her sobs instantly. He had to remain focused on what he was going to do to those two idiots if they were messing with his agenda; he did not want to alter his timetable right now. *I will not fall to those elves and their allies again.*

“I told you to keep the sword in its sheath, or this would happen,” a soft voice said from the workroom.

“Hey, I just wanted to make sure that the blade was covered in enough shadow to hold the enchantment, Ril,” a second, almost identical voice answered. In the background, the sound of sobbing—an almost agonizing cry of pain and suffering—could also be heard. It was quite soothing.

Raer’dreth entered his workroom with his hand in the air, using two fingers to swirl in an intricate pattern. He dropped a spell of silence upon the two speakers and the body on the ground, near a large marble table. The room was large, with a marble table in the center and three high-backed chairs around it. A massive circular hole in the ceiling showed the brilliant night sky, shielded by an invisible spell that kept out the elements, yet allowed him a gorgeous view of the fathomless stars above. Other, smaller slabs lay around the edges of the room with dark armored bodies on them, as well as dozens of crystal stands with soul gems on them; two of the stones pulsing slightly. The archmage stared at the two speakers for a good, long moment before continuing, just to let them panic a bit; they had undoubtedly deserved it.

Ril and Xil were half-elf twins, born of a dark elven father and a human sorceress; identical twins at that. Among elves, twins were rare enough, but to have half-elven twins was unheard of. Both had darkened skin, ice-blue eyes, and faded white hair cut short. Raer’dreth kept them around—even though he questioned his judgment on that choice daily—because of their unique power to see the weaves of future outcomes; both half-elves were prophets. Those beautiful ice-blue eyes could see the patterns of the past and future. As such, they could weave prophecy around a being so that certain circumstances could be averted; handy, to say the least, when you wanted to bring the world groveling to its knees.

Raer'dreth sighed dramatically, a grim smile playing on his lips. They may be idiots at times, but they were his idiots.

"Now that I have your undivided attention, children, I want to know what in the deep hells is going on here tonight?" the archmage asked calmly as he made a fist with his other hand, dispelling his own magic. The sound of the body near the twins echoing in the chamber once more started moaning in despair and agony, writhing back and forth, trying to escape whatever pain it was in.

The two half-elves looked at each other and then started speaking at once, but stopped when they saw the look on their father's face. They turned to each other with a serious look in their eyes and shook their hands up and down, displaying a hand gesture on the last shake...a popular way to settle arguments between the twins; Sword, Spell, Shield.

Rill beamed as he showed Spell, and his twin showed Shield; it was a win for sure. He stepped forward, bowing humbly. "I'm sorry, Father. We thought to enhance the blades of your creations before they were sent to the mainland at dawn," the half-elf admitted.

Xil slapped his brother on the back of the head. "No. *You* thought to do that. *I* said it was a bad idea without father's acquiescence." The two were always vicious to each other; each vying for the favor of the most powerful archmage in history, if they only knew he loathed them both equally.

"Enough!" Raer'dreth brought his hand down in a sweeping motion as his fingers made small patterns. Onyx tendrils of ash came snaking out of his hands, slithering through the air, and choking the twins as it poured down their throats. The spell easily bashed their shields aside; the feeble wards were nothing compared to his power. Once more, he made a fist, canceling the magic as they gagged and coughed for air, falling to their knees. They spat out ash and coughed up black smoke as they tried to regain some composure, failing miserably.

Raer'dreth noticed the Shadowblade lying on the ground next to one of his human slaves; a small cut—only a finger width—showing on her arm. The area around that cut had already turned black and inky tendrils crawled their way through her veins to her heart. The slave trembled with pain, crying softly, desperate to stop the inevitable consequence of the shadow magic eating at her from inside. It would take a long while for the rot to reach her heart and claim her...and he had not the time to savor her suffering; his warriors would be departing in a few hours.

"I want those weapons put back on the host bodies and left alone," Raer'dreth said calmly as the twins struggled to their feet, leaning on each other out of necessity. The archmage crooked his finger and sent another tendril of ash into the slave's mouth, silencing her as it wormed its way into her lungs. The body writhed and kicked as the life faded, fighting for air that would never come, then it was quiet once more. "My warriors will need those swords to enhance their powers and call forth the shadow magic I've bestowed upon them. Once they accomplish their tasks, you may experiment on their blades till the cats come home." Raer'dreth walked by the twins and sat in a high-backed chair, crossing his legs. He smoothed out his ceremonial robes and leaned his head back. It was going to be one of those days.

"Do you want us to work on any other knights yet, Father?" Xil asked with a note of apprehension in his voice.

Raer'dreth knew that weaving patterns around people was time-consuming, and it took the twins almost a year to work on the two warriors who would be leaving. "Not yet. The two you prepared should be enough with what you did to them." Raer'dreth waved them away, dismissing them as he closed his eyes. His warriors were the stuff of myth and nightmares in this day and age; they would not be stopped this time around. Raer'dreth wasn't taking any chances his time around; his enemies would find themselves isolated and alone. He had even made a special amulet for one of them to find the hidden faerie villages and track those elusive creatures. He shook his head, coming out of his reverie, and noticed that the moon was low in the dark sky above, and he knew that the dawn was only hours away.

Well, I'm awake and already here...I might as well start early, Raer'dreth thought as he started weaving the complex gestures of the spell that would send his warriors to the mainland. Opening a doorway to somewhere else was easy, but not if you weren't going with them. Sending someone else was hard, not for someone of his caliber, though. He wove his hands in the complex sigils needed to see over vast distances and never noticed his children share a look and leave, smiling to themselves.

Raer'dreth had waited centuries for this moment, and nothing would stand in his way now. The elves and humans would fall, and he would glory in their suffering. The portal opened, and he summoned his first warrior off of the slab, sending him to the Forest of Tsir. Once that warrior was gone, he cast again, opening another portal to the northern coast of Lorant. It was finally time to bring destiny to heel.

Once they were both on their way, he opened a viewing portal and watched his warrior in the forest lay waste to the faeries with a smile on his dark lips. He didn't watch long, switching the view to Lorant to see his other warrior meet with one of his sorcerer spies. This particular deal would see the treaty dissolved between Lorant and Tsir'illia and get him bodies for his other warriors in slumber so that they may go forth as well and burn the cities to the ground. Raer'dreth chuckled as the sky above him lightened with the coming dawn, the sun just starting to lighten the sky before it could be seen. Far below, his people chanted his name in their songs of the morning, a call to their God who sits in darkness. *Things are finally going my way,* he thought as he walked back to his room.

Forest of Tsir, Northern Tsir'illia

Syn'ella fled through the ancient forest, branches scraping her tiny face as silver tears fell from her wide, golden eyes. Her heart was pounding in her chest as she ran on, goaded by the dread of what was coming for her; coming for them all. Tripping down the riverbank, she hovered for only a second before hitting the edge of the water, her burnt wings flapping despite the pain it caused. She splashed down as her long golden hair fell in her face, covered now in brackish water and mud. *I've got to get away,* Syn'ella thought, her body shaking with fear.

"Come now, sprite, there is no escape," a deep voice called out from behind her. The figure walked calmly, stepping around the rocks and fallen trees like it was sightseeing, rather than perpetrating a massacre. "You're only delaying the inevitable by running."

Syn'ella stifled back a sob, desperately looking around for a place she could hide. *No use,* she thought. *He would only sniff me out anyway, like he did the others.* Syn'ella had been shocked when this creature just *knew* where a faerie was, even when they were hiding, turning at the last minute like he could smell them. She ran down the river, her light frame barely making prints in the mud as she skirted the edges of the rushing water; the benefits of only weighing one stone. *I have to escape and warn the queen; else the entire nation of Tsir'illia will fall to this monster.* A loud splash drew her out of her thoughts, and she risked a look behind her as she ran.

The being stood waist-deep in the rushing water, its burning eyes staring right at her. It *appeared* human, yet nothing else about its mannerisms lent any credence to that description. Shaped like a man, its black armor seemed almost like smoke as it flowed about him. Twin pools of liquid fire burned within its black-horned helm, while raven-black hair cascaded across broad shoulders. Yet the worst part was the smell of magic about the creature.

Humans shouldn't be able to cast magic without enchanted stones and words of power, yet this thing had done so, sending tendrils of ash and shadow throughout her entire village with only a sword swing. The dark magic choked and burned every faerie it came into contact with, throwing their broken, burnt bodies aside like twigs in a storm. The faeries had fought valiantly, gathering against the menace as the young had tried to flee. Even though they were fierce Warriors of the Thorns, this creature bested them easily, sending his dark magic after the fleeing children and slaying them in the span of fifteen breaths; it was horrifying.

Only Syn'ella had escaped the horrid destruction, though she had balked at the prospect of flight at first. She had wanted to stay and fight, yet someone had to get word to their queen. Another faerie had thrown himself at the thing that resembled a man and yelled for Syn'ella to flee, sacrificing his life for her chance. She had still been ravaged, yet his death bought her the time to get out; still, the monstrosity came on.

Syn'ella turned and fled from the oncoming being once more, exhaustion starting to set in as she pushed her tiny body to the limits; she wouldn't be able to outrun him. *There has to be another way*, she thought as she scrambled up a steep bank, her body slowly becoming covered in mud and fallen leaves. Syn'ella rolled into the bushes, tried to stand, and fell to one knee. That's when she saw the ring of mushrooms. *Yes!* Syn'ella thought, knowing that those may just have saved her life.

Mushroom rings were old magic, from before the Wasting War, and could be used to travel to another such ring. The only problem was that if you didn't know where that ring was, well, it was a guessing game where you could end up. Only the oldest of faeries knew what rings went where, and most of the ones Syn'ella knew had perished not less than an hour ago. *Including Syn'valen*, she thought with deep sorrow for her fallen brother. The tiny faerie shook her head and clamped down on her feelings, knowing that distraction could be the end of her.

"Oh, look. She must be tired of swimming," the figure said as it stepped out of the river and walked up the bank, his powerful legs climbing through the thick mud with ease. "Now you get to die all dirty *and* tired."

Syn'ella knew she had no other choice but to take the chance with the mushroom ring, yet if this creature followed, she would just be running again...she had to distract him somehow. "I ask in the name of a Warrior of the Thorns. Who are you?" Syn'ella asked in a voice that sounded like soft music on the wind. She was trembling and tasted the silver tears still falling from her deep violet eyes as she crawled backward towards the mushroom ring very carefully.

"I am your doom, dear faerie, yet that isn't what you asked, was it?" The thing that looked human stopped, planted his sword in the ground, and rested his arm on the hilt; the smoky armor whipped around in the light breeze. "I am Samor Cah, Knight of Shad'ar," the being said with a slight bow. "Now that the pleasantries are over with, may I assume you're done stalling?"

"Yes, I am." Syn'ella's voice shook as fear clutched at her throat. "Now!" she yelled, bursting out of the thicket and pointing behind the being at the river. As the dark knight turned, drawing his sword and crouching, she leaped the remaining few feet towards the ring, vanishing with a soft pop.

Samor Cah was ready for anything...except being deceived by a tiny, insignificant sprite. He screamed his fury at the forest around him as he swung his sword into a sapling, the shadow blade severing it neatly. He had searched everywhere—in all directions—and found no trace of the magic that signified a faerie had passed through here. If there was magic within thirty feet of him, he could sense it; a gift from his unique amulet, his master had gifted him. He could use it to track the magic farther away, but it took longer; she couldn't have gone that far so fast.

All faeries were innately tied to magic, even if they couldn't cast it themselves; they *were* magic. Samor needed to kill this last faerie. It wouldn't do to let his master's plans become known too soon. Once the faeries were taken care of, the elves would fall into despair and attack recklessly. With no more allies and little hope to stand against his master, they would fall. In turn, without the elves, the human nations would crumble beneath his master's dark magic.

How did I lose that troublesome sprite? Samor thought, taking a breath he didn't need and calming himself. The dark knight leaned on a tree and thought about his options. He could just use his amulet to find another village, fueling it with his own life force, but that would leave this one to warn the elves before he finished his slaughter.

What else is there to do? Samor lifted the black stone amulet, the size of a coin, and concentrated. After almost ten minutes of concentration, the amulet tingled as a black arrow shot out in the direction of the nearest faerie. To his surprise, it went backwards, running right through his legs. He followed the arrow to a small ring of mushrooms, the tiny things arrayed in a circular pattern with their white tops tilted inwards. *Of course! These must not register as magic unless they are used, so I couldn't smell it.* Samor shook his head and steeled his resolve. *Well, well. I have you now, little one.*

Being too big to fit into the entire ring, Samor sheathed his blade and eased one foot into the ring. He had hoped that it would be enough, and he was not disappointed. Samor Cah disappeared with a soft pop as he followed the tiny faerie to wherever she had fled. The dark knight had no idea that he was now following a destiny that would achieve the opposite of what he desired—and was created for—yet still bring him peace.

CHAPTER TWO — SO, IT BEGINS

South of the Forest of Tsir, Northern Branthian.

Alant Landsir rode in silence as his lord talked about the Code of the Knights. He didn't really need any lessons on this—already knowing it by heart—but his lord did so like to talk. Alant was a squire in the service of King Danrae of Branthian and was training under a knighted lord. Alant was the first Landsir to make squire in over two hundred years, and everyone thought he would be passed over. No one was more surprised than he was when he was accepted, which he suspected was due to his mother's influence. Alant yawned, brushing his black hair out of his cinnamon eyes, trying to focus. He had been listening to chivalry and honor for most of the very long trip, and almost fell out of his saddle once near the town of Faerin.

"Are you even listening, Squire Landsir?" The stern voice of Knight Joran carried through the open woods. Lord Knight Marcus Joran was a Knight of the Realm and had extensive knowledge of the Code of the Knights. One of the foremost knights in Branthian, Knight Joran was more at home in the saddle than in front of the hearth. He was just shy of six feet tall with short black hair that was graying on the sides and soft blue eyes.

"Yes, my lord." Alant flashed the older man his disarming smile. Alant was also the youngest squire in decades—only sixteen summers this year—yet he was afforded no accolades for this. Instead, he was scorned by his fellow applicants, even ridiculed at times. It did help that he was the same size as most knights already, even at his young age. At over six feet tall and a little more than fifteen stone, the young squire seemed born for the position of Knight of the Realm, and he was still growing. Indeed, Alant had been dreaming of this since his father had told him stories at bedtime of the glorious knights and their deeds of bravery.

"A knight never relies on his looks or charm, Squire Landsir," Knight Joran admonished as he turned back in his saddle. "Batting your eyes at me won't work as it does on the tavern wenches."

Alant nodded solemnly. "Yes, sir, but I haven't really been in a tavern yet, nor truly tried that on a girl."

"Well, I'm sure you will someday, young squire," Knight Joran said with a hearty laugh.

They were on patrol north of Aran'tel city, near the northern Branthian border. The Nation of Tsir'illia—fabled land of elves and faeries—lay past the lightly forested wood they were travelling through. Past these trees, the forest became dense, dark, and foreboding near the river Fae.

Nothing ever came out of—much less went into—the Forest of Tsir. The people of Branthian whispered of dark curses and foul magic, citing that the trees were supposedly saturated by magic, with wild beasts waiting to devour you whole. The ancient woods stretched on for over seventy-five miles north and east, covering the coast of the Irian Sea, and contained ancient towers, hidden villages, and silent rivers— or so everyone said. No one from Branthian had been in Tsir'illia in centuries.

The Kingdom of Branthian was bordered by Tsir'illia in the north and the Endless Wastes to the east. The wastes were a large section of parched desert that rolled on for sixty miles and was the product of the ancient Wasting War between Branthian and Tsir'illia. Legend told of powerful elven archmages battling the human king's army in the verdant forest that used to cover the land. The spell battles devastated the army and ground alike, making all living things growing there wither and die. Within two decades, the land had turned to sand; at least that's what the bards' tales said.

"Knight Joran, may I ask why we patrol the northern border at all anymore?" Alant leaned forward in his saddle as he asked, genuinely curious. "I mean no disrespect, but it intrigues me."

"First, I would like to know *why* it intrigues you." Joran stopped his steed and circled around to face Alant. He always took Alant seriously, no matter how ludicrous the questions.

"Well, we have a treaty with the elves of Tsir'illia, and it's a no-trespass clause if I'm correct." No elf had been seen in over one hundred years, and faeries even longer. *If they even truly exist at all*, Alant thought, staring out through the trees as they talked.

"Correct. The treaty is violated by trespass on either party, yet the knighthood is ever vigilant, are we not?" Knight Joran inclined his head, smirking a little.

"You're right, of course; forgive me." Alant lowered his head, knowing that he had seemed petulant.

"Nonsense, Squire Landsir, you asked a question and learned from it. As long as you do that, you continue to grow as both a young man and a knight," Joran chuckled to himself, some memory running through his head as he looked to the sky. "You were right, my old mentor; I did get a squire just like me!" The knight calmed then, still smiling, and leaned closer to seem less formal. "In truth, squire, we patrol this northern border not to protect Branthian, but to show Tsir'illia that we are still here if they ever think about coming after us." As if on cue, the sound of melodic crying came echoing from the deeper trees. Something was coming out of the forest of Tsir right for them.

As both men looked through the thickening trees, searching for the source of the crying with narrowed eyes, the bushes near them burst open, scattering leaves into the air. Lord Joran drew his sword in a flash, bringing his war steed around to face the threat, keeping Alant behind him and his flank to a tree.

Alant had no such weapon to draw, as squires weren't allowed weapons until they passed their training. He reined his own steed around to face the bushes and saw what came at them. It was no rampaging wild cat, nor was it a host of brigands, intent on their pouches; it was a faerie!

Right out of the pages of his bedtime stories, the winged faerie ran right for them, yet no malice showed in her tear-stained eyes—frantic as they were. The tiny thing was only about two and a half feet tall, stick thin, barefoot, and dressed in tattered clothes. She was caked in mud, and the gossamer wings on her back seemed burnt, hanging limply. The faerie's long golden hair flapped out behind her as she rushed towards them, heedless of the sword pointed in her direction.

"Brave knight, I beseech thee in the name of honor, help me!" she cried, her voice sounding like the tinkling of bells in a storm. “It comes for my life!” The faerie stumbled on, exhaustion plain to both men as they looked on.

Alant dismounted and ran to meet the faerie as his lord brought his horse around between the forest and his new charge. The faerie had called for aid, and no threat would touch her now, while Lord Joran drew breath; such was the honor of a Knight of the Realm. Though this was a clear violation of the treaty, the call for aid for life took precedence over everything. Any repercussions of treaty violations would be for the king to decide.

“To me, faerie, I’ve got you,” Alant called, catching her as she fell into his arms. *She weighed almost nothing*, he thought as he stood and brought her to his own steed. He could feel something pass through her into him, and it was evident on her tiny face that she felt the same; a spark of something he had never felt before.

“Thank you, brave knight.” The faerie shuddered and sobbed into his saddle as Alant covered her with a blanket from his bags; her sniffles made his heart wrench.

“I am no knight, fair creature. My name is Alant, a humble squire of the realm. What may I call you?”

“My name is Syn’ella.” She sat up suddenly as if remembering something. “We must make haste; it will still be coming for me, I’m sure of it.” The sound of fear in her lyrical voice was palpable and made the hair on Alant’s neck stand up.

“Who comes for you, faerie?” Lord Knight Joran asked as his eyes watched the dark forest border whence she emerged. He had his sword in steady hands and looked the epitome of the regal knight standing against all odds.

“A being that resembles a man in appearance, yet is a creature of pure evil. It destroyed my entire village mercilessly and hunted me through the forest. I escaped by the sacrifice of my brother, and I used an ancient portal to come here...wherever here is." Syn'ella slumped back down again, sobbing quietly. "They're all gone...my whole family."

Alant's heart broke at the sound of the tiny creature's voice. He couldn't imagine the pain that this frail creature was in. *The stories say faeries are tricksters and malicious, yet she seems so sincere, valiant, even.* He noticed that she had a sword strapped to her waist, very slim and almost invisible to the naked eye. The thing had to be barely a foot in length. "Are you a warrior, Syn'ella?" Alant asked with apprehension in his voice.

Syn'ella wiped fresh tears away and sat a little straighter. She seemed to gain strength from the question. "I hold the badge of a Warrior of the Ninth Thorn and have earned my slim sword by valiancy in action," she said as if he would know what that was. She looked at him and smiled, "Sorry, yes, I am a warrior, yet this being was beyond *any* of us."

"Couldn't you use your magic?" Alant had always heard the stories of elven magic and the faeries they lived with. It was part of the stories he loved almost more than the knights' bravery.

"Faeries can't actually cast magic unless it is to make themselves blend in. We tried to hide like that, but he could sniff us right out." Her eyes went wide as the very air seemed to change, a pulse like thunder silently concussing in the very ground. "He has found me!"

"Something comes." Knight Joran's tone was low and steady, yet laced with something Alant had never heard before...uncertainty.

The young squire looked to the forest and saw the figure emerge. It did indeed walk like a man, dressed in armor and all, yet there were things that lent credence to the faerie's description. The black armor it wore looked unnatural, seemingly fashioned out of smoke, whisking away on the light breeze. The thing's helm, too, seemed out of place, twin orbs of fire shining brightly even at this distance. The being was well over six feet tall and strode towards them without pause, heedless of the fact that a Knight of the Realm—mounted at that—barred his way with a drawn sword.

"Stand fast and name thyself, being of the dark!" Knight Joran called out, brandishing his sword in the sun's light. His armor creaked as he readied himself for the coming battle, his back straight and his voice steady.

"Move or perish, knight of old bones," The dark knight replied, its voice as wispy as the smoke its armor was made of. It drew a sword as well; it hissed coming out of its sheath as though it scorned the sunlight. "I only want the faerie...for now."

"A Knight of the Realm stands in your path, foul creature; you may not have what you seek whilst I draw breath." Joran sounded less sure now, a note of fear edging into his steady voice. It was the first time Alant could ever recall hearing it.

"Well, that is easy to remedy, ignorant knight." The being never stopped striding toward them as it issued these words. "Yet, I am compelled to give fair warning to an honorable foe. Prophesy tinged with dark magic surrounds my fate and, as such, no Knight can ever hope to wound me in battle." The being swung his sword with a fury, clashing with Knight Joran, relentlessly pushing the attack.

Alant saw the two knights meet, swords clashing and ringing out like twin calls to the gods. It took less than a minute for Joran to be unhorsed as ash sprayed from the sword and burned the animal badly enough to throw Joran. The knight scrambled to his feet and set his stance while brandishing his blade in defense. "I say again, creature. In *honor*...name thyself!" Joran swung with two hands, coming down and meeting the dark-armored man's sword with a clarion call of steel.

"Honor...the one thing that can compel me still," The dark knight growled, almost like it was being forced to answer. "I am Samor Cah, Knight of Shad'ar, and am older than ancient in your eyes." It swung its sword like it weighed nothing, knocking Joran's sword out wide and stepping inside its reach, slamming his head into Joran's helm and denting it in. "I've had more training than ten knights and centuries to perfect my skill; only *Light* may stop me." The blow staggered the lord knight, and Samor followed up with a thrust into the knight's shoulder plates, the steel finding the crease and sliding into the arm beneath. "Yet, because you challenge me in honor, I won't use the magic of my blade to slay you as I did with the faeries; be thankful for that at the least."

Joran cried out, backing up and regaining some balance. He had his sword in one hand now, still keeping himself between the dark knight and his charge. The Knight of the Realm was using the trees as cover while he assessed his fearsome opponent. "Landsir, I transfer the charge of protecting this faerie to you. Begone from the field whilst I hold this creature here. That is my last order and wish as a Lord Knight of the Realm."

Alant wanted to move, but the battle between the two knights held him transfixed in place. The young squire knew the outcome of this battle was something he needed to see—to witness the stand of Lord Knight Joran—yet he was given an order. "On my life, Lord Knight Joran," Alant finally replied, turning to leap into the saddle. The deep voice of the dark knight froze his hands as it addressed him this time.

"You won't get far, boy. This knight won't last long against my skill." The dark knight batted Joran's sword away a second time. This time he didn't step in, but kicked out, folding the valiant knight with a tremendous blow to the midsection, caving in his armor. A quick thrust with his foul sword ended the life of Joran, the sword going into the man's chest to the hilt and out his back in a spray of blood and shadow.

"No!" Alant yelled. All thoughts of self-preservation gone, the young squire rushed the dark knight while it was pulling its sword from the dying lord on the ground. Alant lowered his shoulder and rammed the foul creature, his weight—and the surprise of the attack—catching Samor Cah completely off guard. They tumbled to the ground, the young squire punching and kicking relentlessly as Samor struggled to regain his footing. Alant felt his fists hitting supple material, not metal, yet harder than any leather he had known. *I have to get through this armor,* Alant thought frantically, thinking of the dark knight's helm. The helm wasn't made of steel either, yet when Alant tried to remove it, he found it stuck fast.

"No!" Samor attacked furiously when his helm was grabbed, almost in a panic. The fists of the unholy creature felt like hammer blows to Alant's ribs, and the young squire rolled away, trying to get to his feet. The black knight rolled as well, bringing his sword around and slicing Alant's cuirass, cutting into his chest.

Samor Cah stood, grabbed Alant with one arm, and tossed him a good ten feet to land against a tree with a resounding thump. "Fool! I have already said that no knight may wound me." The Knight of Shad'ar turned and strode towards the faerie, a glint in his flaming eyes. "Where were we, my dearest faerie?"

Alant fought the darkness threatening to take him and crawled to the body of his lord, Joran. The man was dead, yet his sword was there. Alant grabbed it up and limped towards the thing that looked like a man, intent on protecting the charge laid upon his honor. The cut on his chest wasn't even that deep, yet he felt like he was dying already, the pulse of the wound matching his footsteps.

Samor stalked towards the faerie, his gait slower now. "Don't worry, little one, your death will be painless and quick; I have need of your silence." The dark knight reached his hand out to grasp his prize when a sword burst through his chest, spraying the faerie with liquid shadow. He grasped the blade in his armored hands, amazement clear in his voice, "But...how?"

"I am no knight, black heart," Alant spat, Joran's sword steady in his hands as he leaned into the thrust, forcing the dark knight down to his knees.

"This won't stop my master...fool, nor will it hinder...me...for long." Samor Cah fell to his side, the twin flames going dark inside the smoky helm.

Alant kicked the body off the sword and dropped to his knees, the pain in his chest blurring everything. He had avenged his lord, yet violated the strict code he followed by wielding a sword. *Won't matter much if I'm dead,* he thought as he felt a tug on his cuirass. Vaguely, he heard something like music, bells ringing in song. Over and over they sang his name...until he realized it was Syn'ella.

"Alant! Alant!" Syn'ella cried, tugging on his armor. "Awaken before you sleep eternally."

"I hear you, brave Syn'ella. I'm here." Alant got to his feet with a pulsing pain in his chest, the wound from that sword felt hot like a flame. *It didn't feel that deep,* he thought as he peeled off his ruined cuirass and beheld the wound itself, the sight making his blood run cold.

"Amara's leaves!" Syn'ella exclaimed, making the sign of the nature goddess, and backing away.

The cut was small, barely a thin line of red across his skin. The wound, however, was black and pulsed with a life of its own as shadows leaked from it in tiny wisps. It seemed almost like a heartbeat, slow and regular. The skin around the wound was already turning black as well, slowly but inevitably being corrupted by whatever the wound was. Inky tendrils flowed under his skin, traveling out to the rest of his chest slowly. "I have to get back to Aran'tel," Alant said, gasping at the pain and feeling his breath shorten.

"Do you have wizards in that city?" Syn'ella asked as she flew around to steady him as he tried to walk towards his steed.

"No. Wizards are outlawed in Branthian. We have sorcerers to cast our magic instead." Alant wondered why the faerie didn't know this, as wizards were strictly elven or half-elven, and weren't allowed into Branthian due to the treaty. The histories said elven wizards commanded magic with grace and savvy, never needing words or items, just the right gestures to call upon the aura of magic around everything. Sorcerers were something else entirely. Humans had to use enchanted stones that focused power—power gained from old forbidden words and dark powers.

"Sorcerers won't be able to heal that, though...it's magical in nature, I can feel it pulsing from here." The tiny faerie's brows were furrowed as she looked at him, worry etched on her beautiful, yet dirty face.

"They will have to try," Alant said, climbing onto his steed and gripping the reins tightly as the excruciating pain radiated through his chest and into his back. The faerie was right, though; sorcerers couldn't heal magical ailments. They could heal wounds, but not diseases brought about by magic; it was beyond their ability and powers.

"I'm telling you, that wound will kill you before they can even *try* to help. We have to go to the city of Dyln'ir." Syn'ella looked up to the sun and then looked out beyond the trees to the east. "It lies some miles north of the border to the Endless Wastes. If I'm reading the sun right," she pointed to the northeast, "We will arrive in a day or so. Faster if we push this stead to his limits." Syn'ella flew over to the horse's ears and whispered something to the animal, then patted it gently.

"You are unsure of where you are?" Alant asked, trying to keep his mind off the blackness throbbing in his chest as he held on to the reins of his horse.

"I am from the far north of Tsir'illia. We appear to be at the southern border, correct?" She answered as they rode like the wind itself.

"Yes. You are indeed far from home. Pray, tell me, did you flee all that way on foot?" Alant's vision was blurring now, but he had to keep going, especially now that he had a destination. Luckily, he had a good horse to get him there quickly, and whatever the tiny faerie had said to the animal had given it heart, as the beast was pushing itself without Alant needing to.

"No, brave warrior. I took a magical path of chance and ended up here by the fate of Zomnus." Again, she made a sign with her tiny hands—a sign of respect to the God of Luck and Fate. "Now hold on tight. You have saved my life, and I feel I must repay you. Besides, we have a sort of bond I know nothing about, yet I feel it pulling me closer to you by the minute."

They rode for hours while Alant's thoughts faded in and out. He heard his Lord, Joran, telling him to carry his sword with honor, then another time he beheld his mother, asking him to please arrive safely in time for supper. The visions came and went like fever dreams, relentlessly taunting him onward in a blur of voices and memories. Lastly, he heard a voice unlike any he had ever heard, a whisper almost, like the wind.

The time to rise up is now, brave Landsir, for you must unite and save them all...with the grace of Light.

Alant marveled at this, yet the darkness bid him come, and he finally faded.

CHAPTER THREE — TROUBLE IN HALSTRAD

City of Halstrad, Northern Lorant

Falgrim hated magic. It wasn't that magic intimidated her—very few things did—but rather, she hated its effect on wizards and sorcerers who used it regularly. They all tended to have this air of superiority around everyone else. That 'I know the secrets of the universe' attitude, which often made her yearn to bury her weapon right between their eyes—and deep. So far, she had controlled herself this day, though it was still early in the morning and she hadn't had anything to drink yet.

She took a deep breath as the sorcerer, Malakath, continued his ramblings. She was trying not to think about hitting him and wasn't doing very well at all. *If only he would get to the point before supper, then I would consider it a good day,* Falgrim thought, sighing loudly.

Falgrim Ironhaft was a dwarf and, as such, had a fuse as short as she was. She fixed most problems she ran up against by hitting them, even when people said she shouldn't—*especially* when they said she shouldn't. She was a little over four feet tall and weighed enough to make her leathers creek when she sat. Her thick hair was done in three long, black braids hanging down her back, and her traveling leathers were stained with a mixture of blood and dirt.

"Are you hearing me, my good dwarf?" the sorcerer asked with an irritated tone. Malakath Hiram was tall and lanky, dressed in robes that seemed a bit too large for his frame and were an awful color of yellow and green. His skin was pale from lack of sun, and his face was covered in tiny red dots—freckles, the humans called them—that brought out his red hair. The sorcerer continued without waiting for an answer, as usual.

"There seems to be an intelligent commander behind the gnarr raids on the merchant caravans," Malakath said, tapping his skinny fingers on his desk. "Eyewitness accounts give his appearance, and they seem to indicate he is a sword for hire like yourself."

"Axe."

"What now?"

"I'm an axe for hire," Falgrim said, brandishing the weapon like a child showing a new toy. "Why didn't you tell me about him an hour ago?" she asked, standing so abruptly that her chair skidded backward and crashed into the wall. "You've been going on about timing, plans, and missives for so long that I was about to pass out from sheer boredom. Now give me that description so I can go fix this problem—permanently." Her smile usually unnerved people, and this time was no exception. She saw him visibly pale and lean backward, fumbling with his papers and trying to shuffle them straight.

"Ah. Here it is. Tall fellow, about six foot something, wearing black leathers, and wielding a black sword. They say he is an intelligent and competent leader. No doubt he is the cause of all the disappearances of late." Malakath sat back, with that look that screamed, 'See, I'm smarter than you.'

"Let me get this straight. Somewhere north of town, there should be a gnarr camp, ruled by a warrior with a black sword, and you're still going to sit there and only pay me twenty shards?" Falgrim eyed him harder, with that dwarven stare that promised imminent physical pain. She would've done it for ten shards, just to help the town and keep the people safe, but she *really* hated sorcerers.

"Oh, my goodness, Um... Well, let me see what we have in the budget?" Malakath said, sitting up and rifling through the drawers in his desk, trying not to seem nervous and failing miserably.

"You have a 'problem-solving' budget?" She started tapping her foot, just because she felt like annoying him, "You've got to be kidding me?"

"What? Oh, well, yes, something like that. It's actually under 'miscellaneous expenses', but it's better known as the Help Fund." Malakath pulled a file out and looked over it, nodding his head. "It seems that we can go as high as thirty-five shards for the service. Is that acceptable?"

Falgrim nodded, spat on her hand, and held it out to him. She saw him cringe but reluctantly take her hand; she shook it, squeezing a little too much. "I'll take it. Half now and half when I bring you the man's head, or would you rather his hand?" she asked, trying not to laugh at his expression as he blanched. "Head it is then," she replied to his sickened look as she accepted the gold shards and folded them into her calloused hand, walking out quickly, lest he change his mind.

Shards were fragments of ore that were mined by her own people for the rest of Lorant—the whole of Alian'tir in fact. There were copper shards, silver shards, and gold shards. It was the common currency among all the races, besides plain old barter, that is. It was what made the dwarves so fiercely independent in the first place...they were the best miners in all of Alian'tir and even Jerix—God of Thieves and Money—knew it.

It didn't take Falgrim long to gather her things since she was leaving her war pony stabled in the village. The village of Halstrad was smaller than most, numbering only about two hundred people, mostly farmers, loggers, and traders. The main road was packed with dirt and lined with rocks; the side streets were, at least, kept up. It did have wooden palisades, just in case raiders got bold, but so far the village hadn't been attacked. The northernmost village in the nation of Lorant, Halstrad, was almost to the border of Tsir'illia, a land of the elves and faeries. No one here had ever claimed to see them—such was their skill at remaining hidden—but that didn't keep the people of Lorant from fearing them even though the elves had a treaty with Lorant. The stories of the elves and their magic were enough to scare most people. At least the people who still believed in them.

Falgrim shouldered her pack and ignored the stares of the people passing by her. Dwarves weren't well-liked nowadays, not after the Brenshin Wars, but this far north, she could at least make a living without too many problems. King Alban Brenshin had gone to war over the dwarven mines that he *thought* he had a right to, but he never counted on dwarven stubbornness. The war brought out the worst in both the dwarves and humans as it dragged on, and only the death of Alban—and the succession of his son Albron—brought an end to the bloody conflict. The dwarves signed a truce with King Albron, with trade agreements set with Lorant, but humanity had a hard time forgetting the brutality of it all.

Dwarves were reckless and violent, not to be trusted. This was what most humans thought, and, as such, dwarves had a hard time finding work away from their mines in the Starsky Mountains. War veterans, like Falgrim, had it even worse. Fiercely proud of their service, they did not hide their insignia marking them as war heroes; they wore them openly on their cloaks or armor for all to see. These dwarves were ridiculed everywhere they went for being murderers or worse. In fact, more than one dwarf was found hanged or strung up with signs denoting them as criminals for their war service.

Here in the north, however, the people were more forgiving and were far enough away from the capital city of Llor that most of the horrific stories were treated as embellishments; it helped that most of them were. Falgrim was used to dealing with wilderness folks like these; they appealed to her more than most city folk did. The only thing people mistrusted more than dwarves were sorcerers. It was why it bothered her, more than a little, how a sorcerer like Malakath was appointed to oversee the village in the first place. King Albron was as distrustful of human sorcerers as he was of dwarves, and the people here didn't seem to like Malakath one bit—another reason Falgrim liked this little town.

Falgrim shrugged and walked down the street, watching some of the people bow their heads and walk the other way, while a few quickly locked their doors. *Funny,* she thought. *It's like they're afraid of something other than me. Have the disappearances gotten that bad?*

In short time, Falgrim was walking out of the north gate, her pack on her back and a spring in her step. She hadn't been home to Xarvan Tor in over two years, instead moving from town to town helping where she could. After a half mile or so, Falgrim moved off the road, trekking through the brush rather than being in plain view. It was more to avoid others than to hide; she didn't feel like running into any merchants with their hundreds of questions today. It was pure luck that she had been traveling this way.

About half the day later, right around mid-sun, Falgrim spotted a gnarr hiding behind a large rock just ahead of her in the thick brush. Her keen eyes spotted the creature well before it could've noticed her—hells, anyone with half a brain could've seen the stupid thing—but if she had been on the road, it would've had the advantage.

A gnarr was a squat, filthy creature that lived off of others. They had long matted hair and gray skin, covered in scars and warts. Their teeth were more often missing than not, and they had an appetite for just about anything. They robbed caravans and outlying farmhouses for what they needed, even taking human slaves occasionally. They weren't truly a problem for any village with a militia, as they weren't organized whatsoever, often fighting among themselves more than anything. Now, though, with this new leader banding them together, it could spell disaster for the folk of Halstrad; those wooden palisades wouldn't help if their numbers were good enough.

The problem at the moment, however, was that for every gnarr hiding behind a rock, there were sure to be five more. So Falgrim waited, standing behind a large tree as she watched for any signs of further movement. Sure enough, a couple of minutes later, she saw something shift over by two fallen birch trees. *The thing probably got bored and needed to move a bit*, she thought. *Foolish*. She stood up, about to charge them and end their pitiful existence, when suddenly one of them screamed horribly.

The dwarven warrior looked over by the road, her eyes going wide. There, in all of his wicked glory, was their leader. His black sword was sticking through the chest of a fallen gnarr; the beast kneeling in front of him. Its death cry ended in a wet gurgle as it choked on its own blood. The large man was apparently displeased with some of his minions as he slew that one and stalked towards another. The good news was that he hadn't seen her yet. The description Malakath had given her was spot on; six feet and a little with black leather armor and a black sword. What the description didn't mention was his long black hair or wide-brimmed black hat. He was handsome, for a human, and it would be a shame to kill him without having some fun first.

Let's not get carried away, Falgrim thought as she eyed the gnarr near her once more. *Have to take these guys out first.* Falgrim hefted her axe and launched out of the brush, charging the gnarr behind the rock. She swung her weapon clean through the creature's neck, hitting the stone beneath, and mentally cringed at the nick that must've been made in the blade. Another gnarr came in at her side, and she swung backwards into its shoulder, dropping the gnarr to its knees, but not killing it. She looked up and saw that the man in black had dispatched another of his minions and was heading towards her. *Better hurry this one up and get ready,* she thought, swinging her axe at the thing's head. The axe sailed right over the gnarr's head as it ducked and ran for the road, screaming. As the gnarr fled, the man in black looked right at her, a wicked smile on his rugged face; this was not turning out to be her day.

Falgrim backed up and shifted her weight to her other foot, getting ready for the black-clothed warrior. He was no gnarr, and she had to be ready for that huge sword. To her surprise, he brought it down viciously on top of the fleeing gnarr's head, and then smiled at her.

"Disciplining your cohort, madam?" the man in black asked, stepping towards her as the body of the gnarr was discarded. "Don't worry, I'll make sure they all die after I take care of you," he said, stepping in and swinging his sword across her chest.

The attack was meant to test her reaction. Falgrim knew this because she had done it a hundred times to her own opponents. When she blocked the strike with the haft of her axe and twisted, he let go of his sword with one hand and let it swing wide, using his feet as a pivoting point. He spun clear around and grabbed the sword with two hands once more, momentum making the weapon even deadlier.

Falgrim was a little confused, but saw the move for what it was just in time to throw herself to the side ungraciously as he came down with that gathered momentum and slammed the ground where she used to be; the man was good. Falgrim gripped her axe and rolled towards him, coming in on one knee with a vicious swing. Their two weapons clashed in a massive ring of steel as he brought the longsword around in time to block her axe.

They went back and forth, stamping and parrying, neither side giving ground. There were a couple of openings that Falgrim was surprised he didn't take—most of them she left open on purpose—and she started to get a gut feeling that something was off; her gut was never wrong. In fact, it had saved her life more than once in the Brenshin Wars, and she wasn't about to ignore it now.

The man spun and lowered his guard as they broke apart for a breather, eyeing each other for weaknesses. "Ho! The gnarr leader is a skilled warrior, it seems," the man in black said, his words forced through labored breathing as he looked her up and down. "With a heaving chest like that, I think I see why they listen to you." He thrust his sword at her again, trying to catch her off guard, and forced her back.

Falgrim swallowed back an angry retort and tried to focus on what he was saying as she beat his sword to the side with her axe and shouldered him hard. The blow staggered him, pushing the man a couple of feet, and she stepped back to give them some room. *Think, past your anger, girl...something is definitely wrong,* she thought. Then it hit her...this man thought *she* was the gnarr leader! Falgrim laughed and planted her axe on the ground, leaning on the haft as she breathed deeply. The man was good, and it had been a long time since anyone had given her a real workout like this.

"Wait a minute, blackie...I'm not the gnarrs leader, you are. Or, at least that's what I've been told," Falgrim said, eyeing him in case he came at her again. "Got eyewitness accounts and everything," she finished, still ready to fling the axe up with her foot and push it right into his face if he didn't stop.

"Eyewitness accounts…wait a minute, that sounds all too familiar. Did you speak with Malakath of Halstrad?" the man in black asked. "He hired me to rid the gnarrs of their fierce dwarven leader. I'm only getting paid forty shards, but I don't care about the money if it's going to help the village…"

Falgrim didn't let him continue, "Forty shards!" she screamed, spinning and burying her axe into the body of a fallen gnarr. "That double-crossing, arrogant, son-of-a-gnarr!" Falgrim lifted the body right up with her axe still in it and slammed it down once more to free her weapon, and then spun back to face the now startled man in black. "First. What in the hells is your name, stranger?"

The man slung his sword on his back and extended his hand in greeting. "Anatarn Blackblade," he said, smiling. The man seemed just as out of breath as she did, but his humor never once faded. He looked back at the road and shook his head slowly. "So, what do they call you, milady?"

Falgrim clasped his arm and felt a weird shock run through her hand, but ignored it. "Lady? Ha! They call me

Falgrim, and they never use the term lady." She smiled despite the anger burning in her chest; she liked this one's spirit. Falgrim let go of his and looked down, finally noticing the gnarr's spilled pouch. It must've emptied when she split him in two. She bent down and grabbed a handful of shards and a small note. "Here, you read this," she said, shoving the note at Anatarn as she counted the shards.

Anatarn read quietly and crumpled the note, losing his smile for the first time since she had met him. "You are *really* not going to like this," he said, all traces of mirth gone. "Let's get out on the road and start heading back to town. I'll fill you in along the way." Anatarn walked towards the road and started stretching his legs.

"What, by Gar'heth's beard, do you think you're doing?" Falgrim asked as she stared at him. "Is this some sort of religious thing? Are you going to start waving your hands in the air or something?"

"I'm stretching so I don't cramp up from the long run back to the village," Anatarn said, smiling devilishly. "Because once you hear the news, we'll be running most of the day, and I don't want to be left behind."

"You need to stretch before you run?" Falgrim teased, knowing that anyone running for that long would indeed be tired; dwarves were the exception, they rarely tired at all.

"Only when I'm racing an angry dwarf," Anatarn said with a grin. "Malakath paid the gnarrs to kill us both to keep us out of the way. It seems he has been sacrificing townsfolk to appease a dark knight who's now headed for the Capital..."

Falgrim's smile transformed into a death's head grin, the gesture never touching her cold eyes. "He's dead." Her legs were moving like the inevitable landslide off of a mountain in an instant, the powerful muscles sending her along like a runaway mine cart. Dwarves weren't the fastest creatures, but they never seemed to tire. An old saying referring to holding grudges is that dwarves could run until they weren't angry anymore, meaning forever. "I'm going to rip his spine out and use it as a whip to beat his dead, limp body!" Falgrim cried out as she took off. She had never been this angry before—well, at least in the last ten years or so—and by all the gods, this wizard was going to pay.

South of the city of Dyln'ir, Southern Tsir'illia

Syn'ella sat behind the brave human, her tiny arms holding his waist as they rode; she couldn't keep the concern off of her face. He was badly wounded by something vile and dark, and all because she asked for help. She was also pretty confused as to what had happened when they had touched; that spark that flew through them had shocked her for a moment, but then everything had happened, and she had more important things to worry about. Now that she had some time to ponder, it lingered in her mind as to what it could have been. In all her forty-two winters on this world, she had only ever heard of this happening with elves and sometimes, humans; never faeries and especially between faeries and humans.

The spark she had felt sounded like the beginnings of a soul bond, a special kind of link between two people who were destined to be together. Syn'ella had heard of the special bond between elves before, a bond so strong that the death of one had led the other to the grave as well. This bond could be ignored, but at a cost that would eventually see one or both of the people withering away. Once acted upon, the bond would bring the two together so close that it was said they could feel each other from miles away.

Syn'ella sighed deeply, imagining such a romantic bond with this brave hero, but she was just a faerie, and too small of one at that. *He could never find me pretty enough,* she thought as she worried once more about the dark wound he had taken on her behalf. None of the stories of this soul bond ever mentioned the faerie race, and because of their innate magic, it was highly improbable that it could actually happen. She buckled down on her wandering mind and focused on the path ahead. She had to get this human warrior to Dyln'ir and save him, ere his very soul be consumed by this darkness.

He'll probably go home and find a beautiful human girl to fall in love with once he's all better, she thought as Alant moaned in his saddle. He was getting worse, yet somehow, he was still holding on. Syn'ella laid a small hand on the warrior's arm, closing her eyes and praying to Amara for help. "We're almost there, Alant, please hold on," she said softly as the towers of Dyln'ir rose on the horizon.

CHAPTER FOUR — STIRRINGS OF DESTINY

Castle Wrath, Isle of Raer'drin.

Raer'dreth slammed his fist down on the marble table and cursed his offspring for the hundredth time. Samor Cah had been slain and sent back to his body, which was supposed to be impossible. Raer'dreth wove his fingers in a triangle and called the twins. *Workroom, now*, he sent across the winds. His words would find them and reverberate in their skulls until they arrived, causing extreme pain. The archmage glanced over at the glowing receptacle that housed Samor's soul and shook his head as it pulsed with the fractured soul. *How could it have gone wrong already,* he wondered. His thoughts were interrupted by the sound of running feet down the stone hallway.

"We're here, Father," Xil said out of breath while Ril came behind rubbing his temple.

"Why has one of my warriors already been slain?" Raer'dreth asked, spinning towards them both, ire flashing across his dark-skinned face.

They both dropped their mouths in surprise, their blue eyes going wide. "It shouldn't be possible," Ril said, slowly walking forward towards the slab that held Samor's pulsating crystal.

"Wait. We both saw a glowing sword as his downfall—true weapon of the elves—and made it so no other knights could harm him," Xil continued. "What if what we saw was his true destruction? What if that sword could slay his soul permanently?" Both twins nodded at the same time as they looked at each other, pleased they had possibly figured it out.

"Well, that doesn't help right now," Raer'dreth said, calming down a little. "Now, both of you are going to find another body and send him back while I look in on our other dark knight," Raer'dreth ordered. He knew they would have a hard time sending him back, but they had to learn; he couldn't do everything around here.

"Can't we just use a dead body near where he was destroyed?" Xil asked.

Raer'dreth closed his eyes and sighed. It was a genuine question this time, at least. "His soul is almost free this time. You could try that if you knew exactly where he was destroyed and scry there, looking for fallen bodies. Since we don't know where his soul is at the moment, we have to do it here and guide the lost soul into something before it is lost." He didn't wait for any more questions as he turned and walked to the scrying pool. He thought about a permanent death for his knights and wondered. He knew a wizard could bring the souls of the dead back, but it was tricky. There were numerous horror stories from the past. *I'll burn that forest when I get to it*, he thought. "Now go and bring him back, let's see how well you two do."

City of Dyln'ir, Southern Tsir'illia

Alant awoke to the sound of chimes clinking in a light breeze, the scent of lilac and vanilla heavy in the air. Sitting up, he realized he was dressed in clothes that were not his own: shirt and breeches of the finest white silk. "Where am I?" he asked aloud, looking around the room he found himself in. The windows were curtained with satin drapes, and gemstones lined the walls in strange patterns. Even the floor was intricately etched with beautiful scenes of flowers and trees.

"You're in Dyln'ir, good knight," a soft voice said, the tone seeming playful, yet cautious.

Alant ran his fingers over his chest, expecting the vicious wound to flare with pain, yet his skin was whole and unmarred under his shirt. He looked towards the voice and saw a woman—an elven woman—sitting on the floor cross-legged. She was wearing a stunning white dress covered in mother-of-pearl and lilacs. She had long white hair entwined with violet flowers that accentuated her deep amethyst eyes—eyes that seemed to dance with playfulness when she looked at him.

"I am no knight," Alant corrected, trying to stand and bow to his host. He sat back down heavily as his legs were still weak and unsteady. "How am I healed? Is this your doing, milady?"

"Not I. It was my husband who drew the dark shadows out of your wound and made you whole once more. I only run this fair city." The woman stood in one fluid movement and bowed deeply to him. "I am Lady Kysen Drial, and I bid you welcome to my city, Alant."

"I have violated the treaty, on grounds of trespass," Alant stated firmly. "Surely I must be under arrest then?" he asked, not completely sure of what happened or how he got here. *And how do they know my name?*

"No, you most certainly are not. You have saved a member of Tsir'illia at the risk of your own life and, we hear, the life of a Knight of the Realm. No trespass had occurred to the queen's mind." Kysen smiled at him as she walked forward, her dress open way too much in the front, revealing her soft, pale skin; it seemed almost ivory in shade. "Any other questions I can answer for you?"

Alant realized he was staring and blushed. "Sorry, great lady. I have never before beheld an elf, never mind one so beautiful." He mastered his manners and cleared his throat, looking anywhere but at her. "How long have I been asleep?" The young squire vaguely remembered that Syn'ella mentioned this place and must've guided him here, for he had no memory of entering the city. He only remembered getting on his steed before everything went dark. *And those voices,* he thought.

"Your words flow like a river, swift and sure, yet refreshing at the same time," Kysen said, blushing a little herself. "As to the time, it has only been a full turn of the sun since you entered the south gate. Rest now, and I will inform Syn'ella that you have awoken." Kysen turned and made gestures with her fingers and hands; her eyes closed in concentration. "She is on her way. You may want to brace yourself, young warrior." With that, Kysen moved towards the door, but shifted at the last minute as if sensing something. The doors burst open as the tiny faerie came flying in, her wings fully healed and propelling her through the air with a speed that shocked Alant.

"You're awake!" Syn'ella hit Alant's chest hard, hugging him as much as her arms could with their limited reach. That same spark arced through him once more, causing them both to stare at each other for a long moment. They broke contact awkwardly and looked away; neither of them noticing Kysen arch her eyebrow at the exchange and taking her leave, trying not to laugh.

Alant recovered first and stood, holding onto the bed for support. "I am awake and healed, thanks to you, brave Syn'ella. I have no recollection of how we got here, such was the pain." Alant saw his old clothes neatly cleaned and pressed and made his way slowly over to them. He was gaining strength quickly and figured he would be ready to leave within the day. "Let me change and then you may show me this grand city you have brought me to." Alant went behind a set of louvers and slipped out of the white silk clothes they had dressed him in, putting on his clothes once more.

Syn'ella blushed and turned around, holding her eyes, then flew over to the louvers and peeked through them every once in a while, giggling as Alant dressed. Once he was finished, they both went out among the grand city of Dyln'ir.

Alant marveled at the grand elven towers as they walked down a white, cobblestone street at least forty feet in width. He couldn't stop staring at the sights of the Tsir'illian city; the young squire took it all in like a child hearing his first story, such was the beauty all around him. On the sides of the wide street were trees, decorated with hanging crystal carvings that clinked musically in the breeze. Faeries hovered by elven children playing in the nearby park, and elves walked casually by bowing and smiling. "It seems like a dream, this grand city," Alant said, scarcely believing his eyes.

"That's nothing. You should've seen their faces when we came crashing into the gate. The guards all drew their weapons and called for the archmage. The minute I introduced you, the archmage's mouth dropped to the floor...it was like he *knew* your name," Syn'ella said, flying next to him. She darted and weaved through the air, happier than he had ever seen any creature. "Now *that* was a sight to behold, a stunned and speechless elf."

Alant kept his thoughts to himself on that measure and looked around, noticing that the elves weren't just being friendly...they were staring at him. *Maybe it has been just as long as they have seen humans as we have seen elves,* he thought with a smirk. That thought made him shake his head; the improbability of being a curiosity to these people. They toured the large city, seeing fountains and statues, finally ending back in front of the healing house.

"Let's go to the lady's keep and away from the surrounding eyes," Syn'ella said, tugging on Alant's hand as she led him on. She giggled as he stumbled after her, trying to keep up with her excitement.

"Lead the way, brave Syn'ella," Alant said with a laugh. "I am at your mercy."

"That is a dangerous thing to say to me, Alant. I may just remember that," the faerie said coyly, narrowing her tiny eyes at him before leading him onward.

Alant bowed to her and followed, intrigued by her sudden change of mood. He was drawn to this tiny faerie and had to admit it wasn't a bad thing; just being near her made him feel at peace. *Then there is that spark,* he thought as they walked. *I have to figure that out as well, but first, I have to get word back to the king.* The two traveled another couple of blocks and then turned up a winding hill towards a grand crystal keep. The elven guards out front bowed and let them pass without question, another bad sign to the squire's suspicious mind.

"Look at you, up and around," a hearty, lyrical voice called from the side passage as they entered the keep. "I am overjoyed we could stave off that insidious shadow from your wound, young knight."

Alant turned towards the voice and tried to hide his shock; the male elf before him was even more beautiful than Kysen had been. This elf had flowing white hair down his back and the most piercing violet eyes that seemed to bore into your very soul. His attire was a white silk robe trimmed with gold and a cloak of diaphanous mesh. A silver sash tied at his waist complemented the slender sword on his hip that swayed as he walked towards them.

"You must be the healer that saved me," Alant guessed, bowing low as honor demanded. "I am in your debt, good sir, and owe you a life service in the future."

"Thank you for your words, kind warrior, but though I did save you, I am no healer. I am the Archmage of Dyln'ir, Ereval Drial. It is most urgent that we speak in private." The Archmage swept his arm out, beckoning them onward down the passage, and followed between them as he talked. "I have heard the description of the creature you faced from Syn'ella, and I applaud your valiancy in this matter." Ereval moved his hands to the left and hooked his finger just so, and the far doors opened for them all.

"What *did* we face, if I may ask?" Alant asked as they entered a gorgeous room. He tried to remember what the vile creature had called itself as he gazed around the room. The antechamber was at least fifty feet high and had a beautiful hearth set at the far end. Tapestries hung on every wall depicting dragons and ancient towers, as well as battles. Expertly carved furniture rested around the room on brilliantly braided rugs of earthy colors. "I think it called itself a Knight of Shad'ar."

"Yes. I believe the foe you battled was none other than the worst of the mythical evils in this world," Ereval said, his tone serious now. "Shad'ar is elven for shadows, so in your tongue, it would translate as Shadowknight." Ereval walked over towards the hearth and a set of chairs.

The name hit Alant like the hammer of Gar'heth—God of Honor and Battle—knocking the breath out of him and sending a chill up his spine as he sat down heavily in one of the chairs. That name had been in the darkest of stories, striking fear into the hearts of little children for centuries. They were supposed to be a myth, spirits of long-dead knights that would inhabit the bodies of the fallen and take them as their own, transforming them into what they once looked like through dark magic. They were impossible to kill and always kept coming. Very rarely was there ever a happy ending in any of the stories dealing with Shadowknights.

"Well, thankfully I think I killed it," Alant said, yet swallowed when he saw Ereval frown and knew this wasn't going to be good. He had hoped that part of the story wasn't true.

"These beings aren't truly alive, Alant. Instead, their spirits are fused by shadow magic to a dead body, commanded to commit the most heinous of acts for its dark master, Raer'dreth." Ereval sat in one of the luxurious chairs and hung his feet over one side of the arms. "Relax and have a drink, we must talk of the future."

"Did you get word to the other faerie villages?" Syn'ella asked, fear creeping into her voice once more. She kept looking over at Alant, yet whenever he looked back, she looked away with a blush.

"Yes, I did. Worry not, fair Syn'ella." Ereval hooked three fingers and waved as a goblet floated over to him, the fluid inside softly splashing near the rim but not quite spilling. "Alant Landsir, are you familiar with the Silver Concordant?" Ereval asked as he also sent a glass floating through the air toward the young squire.

Alant was taken aback, first by the casual acts of magic he was witnessing and secondly by the ease with which this elf spoke his full name. He hadn't even told Syn'ella his surname. "No, I can't say I have. What is it?" he asked as he took the drink cautiously. Alant sniffed the blue liquid inside and was surprised at the flowery smell.

"The Silver Concordant was the treaty written centuries ago after the war between Tsir'illia, Jal'rien, and Branthian. The war ended with the banishment of the dark elven archmage, Raer'dreth, who had betrayed the elves and destroyed the entire nation of Jal'rien—what you call the Endless Waste." Ereval took a deep drink of his goblet and continued. "Though they had stopped fighting, the hatred between the human king and the elves was still heated, so the two queens added their own clause. Branthian's queen had the power of foretelling, so it is said, and prophesied the return of this dark elven wizard. The queens both added the following addendum at the bottom of the Silver concordant." Ereval cleared his throat and closed his eyes.

'When the knight of shadows falls to the sword of a boy, the elves must give him their Light, and the humans their banner; only then can the Landsir rise and find Dark.'

Ereval took another sip of his drink and raised his goblet towards Alant. "You, Alant, are this addendum."

"I... but..." Alant looked down at his as-yet-untouched drink and drained it, getting a sinking feeling in the pit of his stomach that had nothing to do with his wound.

"I *knew* you were a hero!" Syn'ella exclaimed, fluttering in circles around the archmage's chair.

"I am only a squire..."

"You have bested one of the most vile, evil creatures this land has ever seen on the field of battle. Do not take lightly the hand of fate," Ereval said in measured tones.

"So, what does this mean?" Alant asked, setting his goblet down on an end table made of marble. "Will that thing come back?"

"It means that a great evil has arisen in the west and will be coming soon for everyone in this land. Across the seas it will travel, taking the form of our fallen and attacking the very cities where your family sleeps. Unless you, Alant, are ready to battle it and gather heroes to your side, we are doomed." Ereval waved his hands, making the torches blink out one by one in the darkness, yet relight a second later. "Only you may save us all."

Alant steadied himself. He knew that he always wanted to be a hero...a Knight of the Realm, yet this all seemed the stuff of storybooks and legend. "Very well. If I *am* this hero, what 'Light' do the elves have? And what might I even do with it?"

"That would be mine to give," a regal, diaphanous voice said as a woman entered the room. She seemed to be a mix of elven and faerie, and her feet barely touched the floor as she glided towards him. She had long white hair that spilled down over large gossamer wings on her back and held a staff with a glowing red ruby on the end of it. In her other hand was a golden sheath, gleaming in the flickering light of the room.

"I am Queen Tolandra Asil, and I am here to fulfill our part of the Silver Concordant."

"I sent for the queen when Syn'ella told us your name," Ereval admitted, a smirk on his face.

Queen Tolandra ignored the archmage and bowed, placing the sheath at Alant's feet, a single tear falling upon its hilt. "I freely give the Light of the elves to you, Alant Landsir. Use this how you will; to save us all," the queen said, keeping her head down.

Feeling the grasp of destiny upon him, Alant was compelled to lift the sheath and draw the blade within. As he grasped the hilt and pulled the sword free, a brilliant light filled the room. A pulse went through him, his very soul clinging to this light, changing him. He knew, as surely as he knew his own name, that this was the sword Ilen'dar, or Sword of Light. He looked to the high ceiling; words came to him from the blade, mingling with his mind. "Rise, Great Queen, I accept this gift and will bring honor to its name. I thank you for your gift and promise to die before I let us all fall to darkness." Alant collapsed, falling into his chair, and welcoming the blackness; at least it was familiar.

Road to Halstrad, Northern Lorant

Falgrim had never been so angry in all of her forty-five summers. She had been fooled before, but never like this; and by a human sorcerer no less!

"So," Anatarn started as he raced after her. "Do we have a plan, or are we going to just barge in and throttle the skinny bastard?" he asked as he braced his sword with one hand so it didn't slam into his back with every step. "The guards aren't going to just let us run in with weapons drawn and kill the traitor."

Falgrim looked over as she ran. "Shoulder. Gate. Then give that note to the guards before they spear us."

"And then?"

"Axe in the spine," she spat out as she put her head down and charged even faster.

"What about his magic?" Anatarn asked as he laughed at her solution.

"Can't cast spells without a spine now, can he?"

"Well, then I'd better get there first," Anatarn said, his voice turning serious once more. "I've dealt with his kind before." At that, he took off faster, his longer legs outdistancing the hearty dwarf.

He was playing with me, Falgrim thought as she followed behind. She had never seen a human with such stamina before. The miles passed quickly, and she watched as Anatarn shouldered through the gate of the village, jammed the note into the stunned guards' shaking hands, and sprinted off again. As the guards read the note, Falgrim ran by laughing at the confused looks on their faces. "Just get ready to clean up after us," she called back. The long run had spent most of her rage, but the ire returned tenfold as Malakath stepped out of his office.

In one of his practiced hands, Malakath was holding the telltale stone used by human sorcerers, yet something was wrong. The sorcerer's other hand was dripping in blood; the man was a bloodmage!

Sorcerers were one thing, using forbidden words of power, but bloodmages were the worst of the worst. They channeled power through stones and words as well, but used blood to power their spells, bypassing wards and even armor as it targeted the very lifeblood of the enemy directly. They had always been made out to be myths and fairy tales, but she knew better; she had seen one before in the war.

Malakath transferred the enchanted stone to his bloody fist and spoke a word of power. "Frostar!" The ancient and forbidden word of power resonated outward from the sorcerer, echoing across the town and into the very bones of the bystanders. A white cloud of frost flew outward from the stone right for the charging warrior in black as Malakath smiled wickedly.

Anatarn dove to the side, rolling by the edge of the cloud that would almost certainly freeze him solid. Still, hoarfrost covered his arm as he cried out and hugged it to his side.

Falgrim cursed to herself as the cloud followed Anatarn slowly, tracking his blood. She saw him roll over and over and try to escape it, his screams of pain the only thing letting her know he was still alive. She narrowed her eyes and threw her axe with everything she had.

"Foolish imbeciles, when Callen Drah finds you..." Malakath's words cut off as Falgrim's axe thudded into his chest, spraying blood all over the ugly robe.

"Shut up," Falgrim said, still running at the bloodmage while sporting her death's head grin.

Malakath's eyes went wide as he looked up at the oncoming dwarf; her shoulder lowered as she charged. "You..."

Falgrim plowed into him at full speed, pushing the axe a little deeper and tumbling to the ground with the sorcerer. Falgrim punched, kicked, and smashed the man relentlessly, trying to end his connection to the spell that would inevitably kill her new friend. The cloud of frost dissipated as her blows snapped his neck and ended his will upon the stone. Falgrim kept hitting him a couple more times, then stood and kicked him in the face for good measure to make sure he was dead.

"All right," Anatarn admitted, finally standing up and rubbing his arm. "You know how to deal with them better than I do, though in my defense, I didn't know he was a bloodmage."

"Damned right, I do," Falgrim said as she brushed herself off. Some of the villagers started coming over and whispering to each other. *Here it comes*, she thought, knowing that the old 'dwarves kill people' hate speech was coming.

One older man stepped forward and bowed his head, taking off his hat. "The name's Halin, ma'am, and I just want to say thank you for what you've done," the man said as she looked around. The others were slowly nodding their agreement, and he turned back to the two warriors. "He was a bad one, that sorcerer, and there was no telling who would disappear next."

Falgrim's jaw hit the packed earthen road. "You don't mind that I killed him?" To say that she was shocked at his confession was an understatement.

"Miss, we knew you were in the war—and probably killed a whole lot of folks—but you always treated us kindly when you came around," Halin said, smiling warmly at her. "It's no wonder that sorcerer had it out for you."

Anatarn came over, his voice now soft and full of wonder. "You were in the Brenshin war?" he asked, staring at her.

"Yes. Second axe, 3rd silver regiment," Falgrim answered as she showed him her cloak and the patch on the collar. She avoided his gaze, knowing that he probably had lost someone, possibly to her very regiment. His response was the second of the day to shock her to her core...

"I was in the war as well. Third hammer, 2nd iron battalion," Anatarn said, beaming with pride. He flipped his cloak over and showed her his own dwarven insignia.

Falgrim couldn't have been more surprised if you had hit her with an elephant on a stick. "Seriously? You fought with the dwarves?" the dwarven axe for hire asked. She knew that some humans had sided with the dwarves and even joined their ranks, but they were rare. This was getting to be one of those stories that got better every time someone told it...If they lived to tell it, that is.

"Yeah, I was married to Grinda Silversmith. I lost her in the stand at Brittleshan," Anatarn said as he sheathed his sword and flexed his arm. The frost was gone now, and he seemed like his arm was fine.

"I'm sorry," Falgrim said, looking at him with new eyes.

"Nothing to be sorry about," Anatarn said, slapping her on the back. "But time for talk later, let's get the body moved and find out about this dark knight,"

"Did you say, dark knight?" Halin asked with a note of worry in his voice.

"Yeah, the note we found said Malakath was helping him," Anatarn answered, lifting an eyebrow.

"Well, we've seen a dark knight talking to Malakath lately," the old man said. "A woman, though, not a man. She took off a day before you two came calling, headed south. She said something about catching an elf girl headed towards Llor." Halin paused, looking at the distant sky, a deep frown on his aging visage. "Something is really off with that one, I'll tell ya."

Great, more complications. I was just starting to feel better, too, Falgrim groaned inwardly as she shook her head. She looked at her new companion and realized that he was ruggedly handsome as well as a canny fighter. *And he likes dwarves,* she thought as she let her mind wander. *This could be a fun trip after all.* Yet he had lost his wife, so he may still be grieving. *Better let him make the first move,* Falgrim reasoned as she looked to the south. This whole thing with bloodmages and dark knights was sending a bad feeling crawling up her spine. Falgrim shook her head and slapped Anatarn on the shoulder. "Well, Anatarn, let's find us this dark knight and rescue an elf."

CHAPTER FIVE — ALLIES GAINED

Road to Ferrin, Northern Branthian

She glanced back at the road behind them as the wagon thundered on, the horses near panic at the evil following them. She was using her magic to keep them from tearing the harness off and tipping the wagon, but even that was pushing it; she knew the fear these steeds felt...she had felt it too. Hylana Brendal took a deep breath and pushed a strand of long black hair out of her face, ignoring the tears coming from her bright green eyes; she had to be strong for these people.

The women and children in the two wagons had fled the city of Aran'tel as the men and the surviving Branthian guard fought to delay the dark evil that had come for them all. Hylana gritted her teeth when she recalled the battle with the dark knight at the gates of that lost city, his sword spilling forth dark shadow magic with no word or stone; it was impossible—all of it. That one knight could devastate so many guards and two sorcerers in so little time was unthinkable. Yet, here they were, refugees, fleeing for their very lives. She closed her eyes and heard the cries of children in their mothers' arms as the wagons bounced and jolted down the dirt-packed road, the wheels holding precariously at this speed.

"Is it still coming?" one woman asked while cradling a newborn.

Hylana opened her eyes and looked over at the woman and nodded silently. She had caught glimpses of the dark knight still riding behind them, its black, smoky armor flaring behind him like a cloak. The sorceress clutched her amethyst stone tightly and took a breath, calming her nerves and focusing her mind on the task at hand to get the people to Ferrin and make a stand against the creature. With what she had seen, the sorceress knew what worked and what didn't; so, maybe there was a chance.

"What are we going to do? That thing tore through a Knight of the Realm and at least twenty guards," another woman said, her voice rising in panic.

Hylana didn't know how to answer the woman, yet she was a royal sorcerer who had pledged to keep this realm safe. "We will get to Ferrin soon, and then I will attempt to take it on once more, whilst you flee south towards Branth with the rest of the town," Hylana said with a confidence she truly didn't have. She had thrown her best earth spells at the thing and barely touched it or even slowed it down. Straightforward attacks didn't seem to bother it much, so she would have to improvise, using the terrain more to her advantage.

"There it is!" one frightened child screamed as he pointed behind them. "It comes!"

Hylana saw the dark knight riding towards them with a speed that astounded her. *He must be riding that steed to death*, she thought. A thought that gave her some insight as to how to slow the dark menace so that they could put some distance between them once more. The sorceress stood in the bouncing wagon and clutched her stone tight. "Diron!" Hylana used one of the words of power, calling to the earth once more, yet not to attack the dark knight. She watched as the road buckled under the horse, sending the rider and his steed tumbling over and over in a cloud of dust. That dust would help her complete her plan. "Dir Ea!" she shouted, the word of power reverberating across the distance and making the women and children blanch behind her. This time, she had called the dust cloud—made up of thousands of dirt particles—to solidify around the horse. The particles swarmed the animal and slowly turned to solid stone, covering the entire animal and the dark knight's legs. The horse, now turned into a statue, fell over dead and trapped the knight to it for a time.

Hylana dropped to her knees in the wagon, exhaustion making her vision blurry. That should buy them time to alert the small town and get some of the people away, as they did in Aran'tel. The sorceress shook her head, took a breath, and fought through the weariness. She could rest when she was dead. *Which may come sooner, rather than later,* she thought as she tuned in her seat as another shout came to her ears.

"There's the town!" a young girl exclaimed as she pointed to the horizon.

Hylana made the sign of Zomnus and prayed that they could save as many people as they could before that thing got here. It wouldn't take that thing long to break free and walk, and now it would be even angrier.

South of the city of Dyln'ir, Northern Branthian

Alant wasted no more time in the city of Dyln'ir, knowing that the land was threatened. He was given new armor—a gift from Kysen that he took reluctantly—and a fresh pack filled with supplies. The armor was a new cuirass, armor of the elves that was light, strong, and beautiful to behold. Alant rode out on his steed, packed with rations and water, the horse looking healthy and hale after its stay in the elven stables. Syn'ella, his faerie companion, was going with him, determined to tell the human king how brave the young squire had been. Queen Tolandra would come to Branth once Alant received the banner from King Danrae of Branthian. Alant questioned how she would know, but the beautiful queen just laughed and answered, "With magic." Alant only asked for one more thing to take along with him—a roll of scented cloth; the elves didn't question his request, giving it to him and securing it on the horse. Kysen herself watched them depart, giving them both a strange look as they rode out of the city.

It was over two hundred miles to the capital of Branthian, and if conditions favored them, they could make it in six days of hard travel. Alant stopped on the second day, where Lord Knight Joran had fallen, and gathered the body. He wrapped it in the roll of scented cloth to take back to Branth for an honorable burial, vowing to tell everyone of his former lord's bravery on the field of battle against an ancient evil. The body of the shadowknight, however, was nowhere to be seen.

"Um...Alant?"

"I know, Syn'ella. I don't like that the Dark Knight isn't here either, but we have no choice but to make haste to the Capital." With the body of Joran across the back of the horse, he rode the steed hard and fast to the south, praying to Zomnus—God of Luck and Fate— for a safe journey. Within an hour, they saw a great plume of smoke rising from what could only be Aran'tel, the northern city whence his fateful journey had started with his lord. Alant was going to ride straight past Aran'tel, headed for the town of Ferrin, but he could not abandon those who could be in danger, especially with the body of the Shadowknight missing.

Shifting west, they rode the last twenty miles following the plume of smoke in the distance. When they were in sight of the gate, Alant's gut wrenched with dread. The heavy, iron-bound gates stood wide open, the guards lying on the ground broken and burned. Just inside the gate was the charred body of another Knight of the Realm, this one burned inside his armor. Slowing his steed, Alant dismounted, drawing his new sword, Ilen'dar, and scanned the walls for any signs of life. The sword in his steady hands shed a soft light and pulsed with life that Alant could feel in his grip.

"Alant...where are the people?" Syn'ella buzzed around nervously, hand on her slim sword.

"I'm not sure, Syn'ella, I just got here, remember?" Alant quipped, a smile playing on his lips. He walked through the gate, sword poised for a quick guard. *Thank the gods my father insisted that I learn the sword from early on*, he thought, shifting his balance as he turned down a side road. Just because squires couldn't wield swords didn't mean they didn't know how to use them. In fact, that was one of the tests to become apprenticed to a Knight of the Realm, and Alant placed highest in his class.

"There!" Syn'ella said, pointing to a body in the road behind a house. She flew over without an ounce of fear—or self-preservation for that matter—and checked the body for signs of life. "Alant, he's dead."

"Syn'ella, be careful." Alant looked at the body and saw the same dark wounds that he had taken from Samor in his fight with the Shadowknight's blade.

"Do you know what this means?" Syn'ella asked, her steady voice showing not one ounce of fear.

"Yes. He's come back."

"We have to check the buildings for survivors," Syn'ella called out, drawing her sword and speeding to the first door.

Alant smiled despite the gravity of their situation. Something about this faerie inspired him in ways he couldn't figure out. It was like he had known her all his life, which was, quite frankly, impossible. "We'll search, but quickly. Time is not on our side, Syn'ella." They made a quick search of the houses and found no one, yet signs showed that horses had fled out the back gate along with wagons. More bodies here were infected with the dark rot wounds, and it seemed that these brave guards had bought the survivors time to flee. Seeing no sign of the arisen dark knight, they kept traveling south, eyes now alert for anything waiting for them in the shadows.

They rode in silence, and the miles went by without incident, yet Alant kept a steady eye on the road. They came upon a broken pile of stone that resembled a horse statue, and Alant raised a brow, but dismissed it for another day. Over the next rise, more plumes of smoke could be seen, and Alant's heart sank. He kicked the horse faster, taking the road to Faerin at speed; once again, he was too late.

The town was awash in smoke and flame, with piles of ash and charred wood lying where the houses used to be. Alant slid off the horse and drew his sword once more, this time the blade ringing out with a clarion call of hope against the despair all around him. As if it were a call to the darkness, Samor Cah came around the corner holding a small child.

"Oh, look, it's the boy playing at being a knight," Samor said casually. He looked perfectly fine, no signs of being mortally wounded at all—his body fully healed by the shadow magic of his foul master.

"Release the child and face me, foul creature," Alant said, trying to draw the black knight's gaze and keeping him focused on him. He was trying to project bravado that he didn't feel, yet he would not give in to his fear. "Your prowess in battle against feeble villagers is most impressive, but I've already killed you once—and I was wounded—care to try me again now that I'm not?" Alant saw Syn'ella fly behind a building and knew she was trying to get to the child. If he could hold this vile thing's attention, then they could get the young one safely away, he hoped.

The dark knight laughed at Alant's brave words. "Oh, you're next; I promise. For now, why don't you come over here and kneel before me, lest I end this one's life before you."

Alant sighed and did just that, laying the sword down carefully as he bent his knee. Once he released the sword onto the dirt road of the village, the blade's light faded. Alant noticed that Samor visibly relaxed, almost like the dark knight knew the sword could truly hurt him. *But how*? Alant thought, as he saw Syn'ella fly up behind the dark knight cautiously, her slim sword out and ready for retribution. "So, vile knight, what is your goal here? I thought you were razing the faeries further north. Or has your *honor* taken a different path?" Alant asked as he tried to stall, letting Syn'ella get within range.

"Speak not to me of honor, whelp. The code I follow is older than most elves. Yet, if you must know, Tsir'illia reinforced their guard. So, I have come south to wipe out the human nation first. Then my lord can land his ships on your coast," Samor answered, tightening his grip on the young child. "Now, cur, I want you to tell this child that you will save him."

Alant looked right in Samor's burning eyes, with a smile that promised vengeance. His fear had fled, replaced now with grim determination. When he spoke, his words were directed to the boy, yet his eyes never broke contact with the shadowknight. “Fear not, little one, I *am* going to keep you safe. Know that you are protected by a Warrior of the Ninth Thorn.”

“I thought you weren’t a knight?” Samor asked, venom spilling from his words.

“He was talking about me!” Syn’ella called out as she drove her tiny sword into the back of the Shadowknight's neck. The dark knight flinched—more from shock than pain—and Syn’ella thrust again, piercing the dark knight over and over, flying in tight circles and slicing as she went. Syn’ella’s brave attack gave Alant the opening he needed.

Alant stood and rushed forward, grabbing the child’s arms, and kicking at the Shadowknights mid-section, pulling the child free from that dark grip, and dragging him out of harm’s way. Once the child was thrown back behind him, Alant reached down for the hilt of Ilen’dar, picking it up with a flare of light, blinding the vile creature.

Wait. Samor said before that ‘only Light may stop me.’ I never gave it much thought then, but what if he meant this sword? Alant’s thoughts were spinning as he gazed upon his opponent. As if the sword heard him, he felt a pulse in his hand—an acknowledgment of sorts.

Samor backhanded the faerie, sending her tumbling through the air. “Foolish sprite. I killed your kind in droves. What makes you think you can do anything against me now?”

“I have him to help me,” Syn’ella answered, her tiny lyrical voice shaking.

Samor Cah turned and swung his blade around at Alant, the black blade humming in anticipation of battle. The dark knight stood proud and terrible; yet, Alant was ready for him.

Alant parried the dark sword with his blade—Ilen'dar flaring with a pure radiance—and spun on the balls of his feet, slashing, again and again, backing the Shadowknight up, step by step as the young child behind him fled crying for his mother.

Samor Cah smiled as blow after blow rang out, his centuries of experience allowing him to bait Alant. The dark knight finally went on the offensive and knocked the sword of light out wide, leaving Alant open. Samor kicked out, thinking to catch the young squire in the chest, yet that move had been done before.

Alant saw it coming and dropped back onto one knee, the kick going over his shoulder. He stood up before the dark knight could bring that dark blade to bear, and drove the point of Ilen'dar into the armor of shadow.

A hideous scream punctuated the air, seemingly coming from everywhere at once. The body of Samor Cah evaporated slowly, like dew after the coming dawn. The wispy shadows along the armor were consumed by the sword of light, and the vile creature's screams faded into the distance, as if from very far away now. The empty shell of a body hit the ground, turning to ash almost immediately as the light faded from Ilen'dar. The silence was only broken by the child still crying for his mother.

Alant stood, his now shaking hands holding the sword of light, while looking around at the ruined town. As he tried to control his breathing, his tears threatened to spill from his eyes. People slowly came out of hiding, awe and wonder on their grime-covered faces. There weren't many left, but it was something, at least.

"You did it, Alant!" Syn'ella cried, startling the people of Faerin as she flew towards him. Gasps and exclamations rang out as some hid again while others stumbled out to see the faerie and their savior. The child, finally seeing his mother, ran to her arms, sobbing uncontrollably, yet alive.

"Not soon enough, brave Syn'ella; still, I think it is gone for good this time." Anything else he was going to say was forgotten as a woman stumbled from around the far corner of the street, her white robes stained by shadow and ash. Her long black hair was a tangled mess as she came towards them, her green eyes wide with shock and awe. Her left arm was burned horribly, but she seemed resolute.

"Are you in league with it?" The woman pulled an amethyst-colored stone from her pocket and held it in front of her as if in defense, clearly unsure of what had transpired.

"Easy, sorceress. I am Squire Landsir, and I serve the realm of Branthian." Alant sheathed his sword at her approach, holding his arms out wide. He had heard stories of the power of sorcerers in battle, yet had never witnessed it firsthand himself. "What is your name, if I may ask, sorceress?"

"Oh, thank Gar'heth," the woman said, clearly spent. She dropped to her knees, tears falling down her face as she took shuddering breaths. "I am the sorceress Hylana Brendal. When that thing came to Aran'tel, we tried to hold it off so the others could flee. Another sorcerer and I tested our magic against the creature, but it was not enough. I was tasked to guard the fleeing refugees south while others kept it occupied; they were no match for its power." Hylana knelt in the dirt, overwhelmed now that it was over.

"That thing pursued us relentlessly, so once again I tested my magic against the vile thing. I fear I was found lacking." Hylana wiped ash from her tear-streaked face and set her jaw. "We were going to send the wagons south to Fort Kaldrin and make a last stand to delay the dark knight, but he showed up before they could leave. I sent an urgent message to Fort Kaldrin for aid, then threw everything I had at him, but he overpowered me and was about to end my life when you showed up."

"You are *truly* brave, dear sorceress," Syn'ella said, flying over and bowing in front of the dark-haired sorceress as she knelt in the ash-covered dirt. "I offer my sword in defense of your realm."

"Are you..." Hylana stammered and then stared up at Alant, looking over the faerie's head. "Did you bring a *faerie* into Branthian?" Her voice was astonished, almost awestruck.

"It's a long story. Let's get the survivors together and make our way to Fort Kaldrin." Alant held out his hand to Hylana and helped her stand as the people gathered around him. He eyed them all and took in their faces—the faces of people desperate for someone to offer them guidance and hope. *I don't want to, but there is no one else here right now,* he thought as he stood straighter. "Gather what you can carry, we leave as soon as we can," Alant said, taking command.

They all worked together, with Alant giving suggestions on what they should take and what could be left behind. In less than an hour, Alant and his companions were making their way to the Capital with two wagons of refugees and some supplies. It would take another four days, but saving the people of the realm was worth the layover, he hoped.

Along the way, Alant filled in Hylana about the elves, the Shadowknight, and what happened to Lord Knight Joran. He included the prophecy and even let her examine the sword, watching as her green eyes widened when she held it.

The refugees talked endlessly to Syn'ella, asking her all sorts of questions about her people and the elves, which they had all been taught were the enemy. By the end of the second day, they rounded the King's Wood—laughing at the stories of the faerie and enjoying themselves—when a long column of knights came into view from Fort Kaldrin.

Fort Alreth, Northern Lorant

Anatarn hadn't ridden a horse this fast in a long while. They had been chasing the dark knight for two days, with nothing to show for it. He was sure they would've caught up to a lone knight by now, as the heavy armor they usually wore slowed down most mounts going on long journeys like this, but there was no sign. Fort Alreth was just up ahead, and they could get fresh horses there—for a hefty price, no doubt—and continue on. *Maybe even get some information on anyone passing by*, Anatarn thought as he glanced at his new companion. He smiled at the scowl on her face, old memories of his past coming to the surface after so long being buried away.

Falgrim was a refreshing visit to his troubled past. Anatarn hadn't been around dwarves since he lost his wife, and he had to admit that he missed their direct approach to damn near everything. He caught himself staring a little too long at her curves and focused on the road ahead; it had been a long time since he had laid eyes on curves that good, and it always brought a smile to his face. *And what was up with that shock when we clasped arms,* he thought as they rode on. *Never had that happen before.* Anatarn had no more time to dwell on that as they came around a bend in the road and beheld a column of smoke rising from the fort. His smile faded quickly with the complete absence of guards or the famed Red Warriors of Lorant.

"*That* can't be good," Falgrim said as she kicked her mount faster, her hair flying out behind her.

Anatarn sped off after her, goading his steed to hurry. A lone figure emerged from the ruined gates and stumbled towards them in a tattered dress of diaphanous silk, her hair a mess of blood and ash; it was a female elf!

"Didn't that old man say something about that dark knight looking for an elf girl?" Falgrim asked as they raced towards the fort side by side.

"Yes, and I'm not liking how this all looks right now." Anatarn slid off the horse as they slowed and rushed to the girl's side. She was covered in blood, none of it seeming to be hers.

"Flee, kind strangers," the elf said meekly, her lyrical voice sounding hoarse. "There is nothing but death here."

"Bah, death has ever been close, elf, and it hasn't stopped me yet," Falgrim said as she brandished her axe. The dwarf crept closer to the ruined gate and peeked in, then backed up as if shocked.

"What is it, Falgrim?" Anatarn asked, knowing it had to be bad to make someone as hardened as Falgrim look like that.

"It looks like the Battle of Horin Tunnel," Falgrim said with a note of sadness in her gravelly voice.

Anatarn drew in a shocked breath. The Battle of Horin Tunnel was one of the bloodiest victories the dwarves had won against the king's forces. They had lured two columns of soldiers to a deep tunnel and then ambushed the humans in the dark. Dwarves had excellent vision in the tunnels, and the resulting slaughter left over one hundred men and women dead, their bodies barely recognizable as they all fell together in bloody piles in the cramped space of the confining tunnel, as the dwarves continued to hack at anything that was taller than themselves.

"What did it? Was it a gnarr attack?" Anatarn asked, trying to wrap his mind around what could slaughter a host of Red Warriors that easily. The Red Warriors of Lorant were specialized warriors, trained to serve the king in all things until death. They weren't your typical knights in armor; instead, they wore gleaming chain and wielded long silver lances with plumes of red on their silver helms. The Red Warriors were notorious for their prowess in battle and had been a thorn in the dwarves' sides during the war.

"No. Whatever did this, it burned everyone as well as cut them to pieces. It has the stench of magic to me," Falgrim said as she walked back to his side, her grip on her axe noticeably tighter as her knuckles whitened.

Anatarn looked to the elven girl at his feet and saw the horrified look in her deep violet eyes. It struck him then that he had no idea how old she was. He had only ever seen one elf in his life and was shocked at how young this one seemed. All elves looked much younger than they appeared—such was the benefit of living hundreds of years—but this one looked truly young. Her disheveled and blood-stained white hair was entwined with ruined lilacs, and her beautiful, yet tattered, white dress was stained with ash and dirt. She wore a golden sash around her waist and seemed to carry no weapon.

She spoke as she stared off into the distance, like she had seen the depths of the hells and knew what was awaiting them all. "It was a Knight of Shad'ar, or Shadowknight...a monster out of myth and legend," she said with her tiny melodic voice tinged with fear and even a little regret. "It came looking for me, and the guards tried to bar her way. The creature slew them easily as the Red Warriors of the fort mobilized against her. Their lances did nothing as the dark knight devastated them with that blade and shadow magic." Tears rolled down her stained cheeks, smudging the ash on her face, as she recounted the horrific battle. "I hid as the rest of my retinue sped off to lure it away south, trying to save me from the wrath of that monster." She broke down completely then, her great sobs wracking her as she shook in Anatarn's arms.

"What's your name?" Anatarn asked softly, holding her as gently as he could. He had a hard time trying to believe that all those stories of Shadowknights were real, but hearing her voice lent them credence. *Besides, I just fought a bloodmage, and they were a myth, too.*

"My name is Eliyan Safril, of the House Safril...Niece to the Queen of Tsir'illia." She held her head a little higher at the proclamation, but still looked exhausted. "I am a wizard and healer, bound for treaty talks with the King of Lorant."

"Well, let's get going then," Falgrim said, holding out her hand to help the elf up on her feet once more. The dwarf had an odd look on her face as she stared at Anatarn, like he was doing something wrong. "If this thing is after you, then it'll be back."

"She won't stop until she kills me," Eliyan said, looking up at the dwarf. "I don't want to drag you into this."

Falgrim snorted, steadied the elf, and kicked a rock with her boot. "No matter to me. I've had a full two days to think about how I'm going to kill that thing. Whatever did this to these people *will* feel my axe by the end of this journey."

Anatarn had to smile. Leave it to a dwarf to make things that simple; it was what drew him to them in the first place, why he fought so hard for them. "Sounds like a plan. It's another four days' travel to Llor, at least." Anatarn looked at the young elf and smiled. "Eliyan, you'll come with us, and we will deliver you to the king safely ourselves," he stated, fingering his sword. "And if this Shadowknight tries to come at you again, well, she is in for a surprise."

“*That* sounds like a plan,” Falgrim agreed, taking the girl’s arm and giving Anatarn one of those looks again. “But she rides with me.” The dwarf stomped off and mounted her steed, leaving Anatarn more than a little confused.

“Lead the way, dear dwarf,” Anatarn said, as he mounted his steed. He drew his blade and rested it on his lap, ready for whatever was coming.

CHAPTER SIX — HONOR FIRST

Just North of Fort Kaldrin, Kingdom of Branthian

The column of knights from Fort Kaldrin was impressive, to say the least. More knights were riding in double formation than Alant had ever seen in one place, and he had grown up in the Capital. The young squire had trained at the fort—sometimes called Knight's Rest—briefly, but had never seen so many ready for battle like this; it was right out of the bards' tales. The knights rode in tight formation and at speed, slowing when they saw the wagons of refugees and Hylana at its fore with Alant.

"Hail, Sorceress Brendal!" the lead knight called, recognizable as Knight-Captain Sarin Marveth. "We received your urgent message for aid on the winds of magic. We ride now to vanquish this creature of darkness." The Knight-Captain pulled up close to them, eyeing Alant suspiciously. "Is it pursuing you still?" The man had grey hair and brown eyes that judged all who he turned his gaze upon.

"Hail and well come, Knight-Captain Marveth. It has been vanquished already by this brave man beside me," Hylana said, tilting her head to the knight and waving her hand at Alant. "He and his faerie companion saved us at the town of Faerin."

"Faerie? Surely you jest?" the Knight-Captain said, laughing and looking back at his men.

"I am no jester, brave knight," Syn'ella said, fluttering up from the back of Alant's horse. Her gossamer wings beat quickly as she drew her chin up proudly.

Alant held up his hand for peace before the shouts could ring out at the sight of Syn'ella. He knew this was going to be the hard part, yet his code as a squire demanded the truth. "It is the truth. I also bring the body of Lord Knight Joran home for an honorable burial. The Knight of the Realm gave his life battling the Shadowknight named Samor Cah, defending this citizen of Tsir'illia."

A chorus of gasps arose from the knights within hearing range at this proclamation, the Knight-Captain drawing his sword with an outraged expression on his face. "And who are you, sir, who professes to slay such a creature of myth when an esteemed Knight of the Realm lies dead?"

"I am Squire Alant Landsir, and I come with a message from the Queen of Tsir'illia for King Danrae of Branthian."

"A squire with a sword? With a Tsir'illian on Branthian soil?" Marveth turned to his knights, sheathing his sword. "Arrest this faerie and bring the *boy*. Make sure he is in irons at that." The Knight-Captain's words dripped with contempt, turning his back on them and riding to the rear of his host.

"Knight-Captain Marveth," Alant called loudly, for all to hear. "Hear the last words of Lord Knight Joran—*Landsir, I transfer the charge of protecting this faerie to you. Begone from the field whilst I hold this creature here. That is my last order and wish.*" Alant slid off his steed, a smile on his face as the closest knights advanced upon him. That would get the man to listen to him at least. Alant knew the Code of the Knights better than most; it was the one thing he was going to miss about Lord Knight Joran and his endless talks and lectures about that book and its contents.

The Code of the Knights was a huge book, located in the capital city of Branth. It was thousands of pages detailing everything a Knight of the Realm would need to act with both honor and courage in everyday life. From there, a knight could aspire to become a Lord Knight and gain his own squire.

As the knights advanced, Syn'ella flew in front of Alant with her tiny hand on the hilt of her slim sword, yet she didn't draw it... "I'll fight by your side, Alant."

"It won't come to that, Syn'ella." Alant gently eased her behind him, seeing the stunned faces of the angry knights at the sight of a faerie with a weapon. "He'll listen to me."

"Hear him out, Knight-Captain. This young man saved all of us, and I saw firsthand the creature he fought. It was beyond even my power," Hylana said, walking her steed forward to stand with Alant.

Knight-Captain Marveth nodded and waved his knights back. "Speak then, *Squire*. Tell me why I should not arrest you and enslave this faerie right now."

Alant saw the other knights looking from their leader to him and back, waiting with bated breath. Alant cleared his throat and stood a little straighter. This was the tricky part, but he was counting on someone as high-ranking as Marveth to know the obscure parts of the code.

"As I am following the last order of a fallen Knight of the Realm, I can only be judged by the king himself—after giving my story directly to him, of course..." Alant let his words hang in the stunned silence, eyeing the other knights carefully to gauge their reactions.

"He mocks the Code!" One knight called out.

"I *follow* the code," Alant said plainly. "As Lord Knight Joran instructed me every day."

A flare of light came from Hylana's outstretched hand, calling their attention. "Squire Alant has the right of it, Knight-Captain. Take us to the king," she said, a smile slowly spreading on her face as the knights all looked at her.

Silence followed the sorceress's words as they all looked to Knight-Captain Marveth. The man solemnly nodded, turning to the knights behind him. "The faerie is in his charge and, because it was the last wish of a fallen knight, no penalties can be accrued by this man until and only when the king so declares. Back to the fort, men," he said, turning to Alant once the knights started turning their formation. "That was a pretty obscure rule, squire. Leave it to Lord Knight Joran to teach that to you." The Knight-Captain finally smiled, clasping Alant on the shoulder. "I trained with Joran in our youth, and he will be sorely missed. Forgive my words of anger; the loss of a dear friend clouded my judgment."

"He fought with honor and courage, Knight-Captain," Syn'ella said quietly, hovering over to the proud man. "Against a foe that slaughtered hundreds of my friends and family. Know that his name will be written in our ledgers as well."

Marveth raised his brow at the proclamation. "That is most kind of you, dear faerie, and I look forward to hearing about his last stand as we travel."

"That would be my great honor, Knight-Captain," Syn'ella bowed and flew back to the horse, landing quietly and folding her wings.

Marveth nodded and then turned to the south, giving a shrill whistle that signaled the formation to move once more. They were on their way, yet even though they rode ready for battle, not one of them knew just what kind of horror would be coming for them out of the dark.

Gates of Rissen city, Coast of Lorant

The dark knight reined in her horse at the gates of the eastern city and surveyed what stood against her. The city of Rissen stood in her way to continue towards the Capital of Lorant and quite possibly guarded what she sought behind its sturdy walls. She had chased those elven fools all the way south to this city, and now they thought these barricades would stop her when the wooden palisades of the fort could not. The dark knight's burning eyes looked up as a horn blew from the watch tower in the eastern corner, telling her they knew that she was there. *Good, let them quake at my power,* she thought.

Callen Drah was a knight of Shad'ar and, as such, was almost invincible to most mortals in combat. She was centuries old—even if the body she was inhabiting wasn't—and her knowledge and skill were far better than the most skilled warrior humanity could hope to send against her. She *seemed* human, with her dark, shadowed armor flowing around her like smoke and long copper hair spilling out from her helm upon slender shoulders; the resemblance ended there, however. Twin pools of liquid fire burned within that black helm, and her voice sounded like the whispers of the grave. "I only want the elven girl, fair citizens of Rissen."

"You will not have that which you seek, foul knight," a voice called out from behind the gate, a note of trembling fear within its timbre.

“You have no hope to deter me, human,” Callen said, her voice raised so that all may hear now. “Yet honor demands that I give you the chance. Know this, though. Prophesy tinged with dark magic surrounds my fate and, as such, no blade may wound me in hand-to-hand combat; only *Dark* can stop me.” She bowed slightly as she drew her blade, infused with shadow magic. They would never understand her honor in battle; not many would, these days.

Callen Drah was raised on honor, as a knight in the service to the long-dead nation of Jal’rien during the Wasting War. Callen and a group of fellow knights had pledged themselves to Raer’dreth, vowing to serve him even after their demise. They rode to battle against their own kind as foul magic destroyed everything they had held dear.

They were renamed the Knights of Shad’ar, and when the dark elven archmage worked his magic, binding them to his service, they became his—even when they perished in battle. Their spirits flew to enchanted crystals, holding them tight from the afterlife until he could send them to another body, their armor and sword following them like a cursed skin. They were enslaved in all but name, having no choice but to do as he commanded.

If we had understood that promise back then, she thought. *I wonder how many would’ve said no.* It mattered not; she had given her word. Now, honor was all they had left of their free will, and if asked their name, or challenged in combat, they could not refuse; they even had to inform their opponents of their weaknesses and invulnerability, such was the pull of their honor. So far, only she and Samor Cah had these prophetic auras about them. However, given time, those insufferable twins could make the others just as powerful.

Callen cleared her mind as the gates swung open to reveal a lone warrior riding purposefully toward her on a magnificent steed. *Another of those lancers, no doubt,* she thought as she looked him over. The man was over six feet tall and carried himself like an accomplished warrior, his gleaming mail and bright shield reflecting the sunlight. His lance was held with proficient skill, and his eyes scanned her the minute he laid eyes on her; pity he would still die. "Did you not understand my warning?" Callen asked as she dismounted and advanced, regardless of the fact that the man was still mounted. She had to fulfill her mission and slay that elven diplomat at all costs, and she fought better on her feet.

The warrior smiled and inclined his head in respect to her, lowering the visor on his red-plumed helm. "I did indeed, dark knight, yet honor demands I fight you in The Rule of One," he said, invoking the ancient rite of combat.

That gave her pause, if only because it was something from her past. If a city sent out its champion and they lost, the city would surrender, but be spared from any other citizens dying. It was clever and guaranteed that anyone would be spared if they were sheltered behind those walls. However, the ancient rite clearly stated that they had to be citizens of that city...her quarry was not. It was a little detail—and one they clearly missed—but it would allow her to complete her task quickly.

The man came on, determined to sacrifice his life for his city; a noble act, no doubt, but still foolish. These humans didn't know how precious life was until they died a few hundred times. Callen missed having a soul that was her own.

Callen let the man charge, sidestepping predictably as he went by, ducking the lance that was aimed at her head. Her sword sliced down the side of the animal, opening it up wide and spilling the rider to the ground as the straps of the saddle gave way. The man hit hard but rolled away from the dying animal and got his feet under him, drawing his backup sword.

He seemed unfazed, yet cautious. Most opponents would've leapt out of the way, not held their ground as the charging animal came at them.

Callen let him advance again, his first attack going straight for her heart. As it struck, Callen felt it bounce harmlessly to the side, deflected by the armor. His second swing, she parried and stepped in close, behind his shining shield. His wide eyes told her he knew his peril as her sword slid effortlessly up under his chain shirt and into his lung, leaking dark magic into the wound at her silent command.

"What..." The warrior fell back, gasping for air that wouldn't come, and coughed up ash as the foul magic from the sword obeyed her wishes. The man's lungs were already rotting, and the magic was spreading quickly to his heart as the ash swirled in his body. He was dead in ten heartbeats.

"Open wide your gates, people of Rissen, and give me the elves you harbor within. Do this and your people may yet live," Callen said, striding forth as she needlessly wiped her blade on the fallen man's cloak. She would have said more, but she was caught off guard as an axe buried itself in her back, slamming into her armor and causing massive damage to the body underneath. "How..."

Falgrim saw the dark knight up ahead and knew the man facing her was as good as dead. It was the way the female knight stood—like she didn't care what he did. That spoke of unmatched skill, and Falgrim had seen that before in her younger days against her dwarven weapon master. "Stay here with her, Anatarn," she said reluctantly as she kicked her mount forward. She loathed the way he looked at the cute little elf, but she had to challenge this foe alone. Falgrim didn't like the look of that confidence whatsoever.

"Falgrim, you can't do this by yourself," Anatarn called after her.

Falgrim was already gone, pulling her axe and charging down the packed earthen road. When the man dropped and the knight walked over his corpse, she had a momentary thought that this was a bad idea, but dwarven stubbornness won out in the end. Fifty paces from the dark knight Falgrim cocked her arm back and brought it forward with everything she had, letting the axe fly. Her aim true, the weapon slammed into the back of the knight, right in the center of her shoulder blades, and sent the dark knight forward to its knees, that shadowy armor rent wide open where the axe had hit. Falgrim heard the knight gasp and call out something, but she was still too far away to hear what.

The dark knight turned and stood, her shadowy blade in her steady hands. Her flaming eyes were bright as she squared her shoulders. "You will pay for that, dwarf. I know not how you managed to wound me, but it will avail you naught." The knight stood, braced for a charge now, and held her sword for a swipe when the dwarf angled the small mount to the side as she rode past her.

It was a good thing Falgrim didn't plan on doing that. "Suck dirt!" Falgrim cried as she threw herself from the mount when they got close, leaping straight at the dark warrior. The dwarf hit the surprised knight like a boulder, and they went down in a tumble, the blade of shadow knocked clean from the dark knight's hand and clattering in the dirt and dust. Falgrim was punching and kicking with abandon, her fists hit as hammer blows upon a forge, and every one of them rocked the female knight.

Finally kicking out and sending the dwarf rolling away, the dark knight rolled and got to her feet, standing straight with her burning eyes narrowed behind her black helm. She held out her hand, her sword flying to her. "You fight well, dwarf, yet my skill is beyond you," she said as she strode forward. "You have no weapon now, and the element of surprise is gone."

Falgrim knew the dark knight was right; she had to stall a bit more. Her axe was a good twenty paces behind them. "What did you do with the people of Halstrad once Malakath took their blood, Callen Drah?" Falgrim asked. The knight's pause was exactly what she was hoping for. "Oh yes. That bloodmage gave up your name easily."

Callen Drah hesitated before shrugging. "My name matters not, but to answer you, the people were sent to my master to be used as vessels for my brothers and sisters in the knighthood."

Falgrim backed up a little more, slowly, keeping her feet balanced and ready for the knight's lunge. She knew the knight would try to stop her from retrieving the axe...in fact she was counting on it. "Well, for that, I'll see that head of yours roll." Falgrim made to leap at her axe as she finished, waiting for the knight to act, but spun instead and lashed out with a powerful kick.

Callen Drah did indeed lunge with her blade, attempting to skewer the dwarven warrior, ere she grabbed her axe—the axe that somehow damaged her when it shouldn't have been able to. The Knight of Shad'ar overextended and paid for it as a foot planted itself squarely into her knee, knocking it out wide and putting the dark knight off balance. Callen cried out in shock, more than pain, and fell to the side.

Her Shadowblade clattered in the dirt once more after the dwarf punched the wrist holding it and ran for her weapon."

Falgrim sprinted the last ten feet and grabbed her axe. She turned as the knight was trying to stand, and threw the axe again, this time aiming for the head. "Die in a hole!" Falgrim screamed, using the worst dwarven curse she knew. The axe hit hard and buried itself in the helm, splitting it and throwing the knight backward to the dirt road. Black shadows leaked from the helm as the flames in those eyes faded. "And stay that way!"

"Sadly, she won't," Eliyan said as she and Anatarn came riding up. "She is a Shadowknight and, as such, her spirit is already on its way back to her master. He will just put her into another body."

"Aren't *you* the ambassador of good news," Falgrim sneered, wrenching her axe out of the face of the dark knight and hitting her again in the face for good measure. "Can we just burn the body?"

"Yes, but it will avail you naught."

"You going to talk like that a lot?" Falgrim asked, already disliking this elf for the way Anatarn looked at her. Falgrim shook her head at the feeling of jealousy rising in her gut and scolded herself. She had never fallen for a human before and wouldn't start now. Besides, she hated flowery speech almost as much as she detested magic.

"Anyway," Anatarn said, changing the subject. "Let's get inside the city and see if her friends are still here. We have to get to the Capital before this thing comes back." He walked by the body and stopped, placing his hand on his sword.

"What's the matter? Feeling down because you didn't get to test your mettle against her?" Falgrim asked, chuckling a little. She knew he was skilled, but wasn't sure he could have done any better than her. She took her axe and severed the head of the knight, kicking it a little so it rolled away from the body; a promise was a promise, after all.

"No, my sword just hummed a bit when I walked by...it has never done anything like that before." Anatarn shrugged and walked on, but Eliyan rushed to his side.

"What do you mean, *exactly*?" Eliyan asked, staring at the blade with interest. "It truly has never done that before?"

"No, never."

"You do know this is an elven blade, right?" Eliyan was bending down now, staring intently at the sword as he held it.

Anatarn shrugged. "Yes. My father was given this blade from his father, and he passed it on to me." The large blade was as black as night and barely reflected light at all. He had always known it was enchanted, as no weapon this large could weigh so little, but beyond that knew nothing about it.

"This is all *very* exciting, but we really have to go before that *thing* gets up and tries again," Falgrim interrupted, tapping her foot impatiently. "I'd rather not test my luck twice."

"Milady!" a sweet voice called out. An elf was rushing towards them in a panic, his clothes disheveled and his eyes wide with fear. Guards followed the elf out and looked at the body of the black knight as others picked up the fallen warrior of Rissen gently.

"You're right, Falgrim. Let them burn it," Anatarn said to the dwarf as Eliyan went to meet her friend. "It will make me feel better anyway."

"Agreed," Falgrim said, taking out tinder and a strike stone. She lit a torch from her pack and dropped it on the body of the dark knight, the remains going up quickly as if by magic, and then she kicked the head back towards the roaring flames.

"Calm thyself, Ongril, I am unharmed," Eliyan said with a pleasing smile as she hugged the elf. "These two heroes found me and brought me to you. I present to you, Anatarn and Falgrim."

Ongril stopped and bowed to both warriors, eyeing Falgrim hesitantly. "I am Ongril Silvertree, steward to Eliyan." He bowed to Anatarn and Falgrim, then turned back to Eliyan. "We were so worried when we set out to lure that knight away...we didn't know what would happen to you." He closed his emerald green eyes for a second and looked up to the sky as if in supplication. "We heard the screams as we fled, hoping to draw the vile creature after us...did it kill them all?"

"Yes," Falgrim answered for Eliyan, her patience running out. "Now, *please,* can we head south for Llor?"

Anatarn laughed when Falgrim rolled her eyes and stomped away to her stead. "This is going to be a fun ride, isn't it?" he asked rhetorically, patting the elf on the shoulder. "It's fine, Ongril, we can talk on the way."

Eliyan turned towards the two warriors, tilting her head. "I have my retinue again; surely there is no need for you to escort me all the way there now?"

"We promised to get you to the Capital...and I *always* keep my promises." Falgrim interrupted as she looked back at the fallen knight, the guards standing near the burning body. "Now, let's go." *That will hopefully slow it down,* she thought as she walked to get her pony. *If not, well, this is going to be a really fun ride indeed.* She mounted the steed and frowned as she saw the elves still talking. It was going to be one of those trips...

CHAPTER SEVEN — DESTINY REVEALED

Castle Wrath, Isle of Raer'drin.

Raer'dreth screamed and hurled his goblet at the wall, the deep red wine splashing all over the tapestry hanging from it. Both of his knights had been somehow slain, working around the prophecy woven by the twins. Callen Drah was salvageable, but something had nearly obliterated Samor Cah's very life essence; a feat he thought was impossible. Raer'dreth could bring him back...but there would be consequences. *A project for another day,* he thought as he went over what he would need to summon the dark spirit from the arms of his goddess once more.

"We can start work on another knight right away, Lord," Xil said, prostrating himself before the archmage.

"Your weavings have done very little so far," Raer'dreth snapped, bitterness dripping from his every word. "What makes you think that another would fare any better?" The archmage closed his eyes and rubbed his temples, a pounding headache starting to form.

“I’m sorry, Father,” Xil said, still looking at the floor. “We only work with what fate gives us; we know not what will transpire most times, just that it is very specific.”

Raer’dreth took a deep breath to calm down; yelling further would do no good. “Fine, but it will take too long to weave prophecy around them. Work to get them set for the bodies we received and ready for the invasion,” Raer’dreth said, his anger having finally subsided. “Besides, I may have just the plan we need to divert our enemies’ attention.”

“Yes, my Lord,” Xil said with his head to the floor. “The bodies from Halstead should be here in time for the launch, and Ril and I will have them all prepared and waiting for the souls to be transferred.”

“Then now we wait for my generals to get the ships ready.” The dark elf stood and smoothed his robes as he walked down the dais of his throne and over to the map on the wall. The map was of the continent Alian’tir, encompassing all the nations, and showed where the key places he needed were. His finger landed at a spot in the middle—the sight of his greatest triumph and his greatest failure all rolled into one—the Endless Wastes.

Ril came sprinting in, out of breath from running. “I told them your wishes, Lord. The ships will be ready to sail in a tenday—all seventeen of them.”

“Ah, perfect timing,” Raer’dreth said as he tapped the spot on the map he had targeted and nodded silently. The archmage waited for Ril to crouch down and prostrate himself as well before turning to them. They had failed him, and they knew how he usually handled failure; good thing he still needed their prowess at casting magic in the battles to come.

“I was saving this little surprise for when my forces had already attacked, but it may well serve as a distraction *before* they get there,” Raer’dreth said, walking with his hands behind his back. His trusted bloodmages and dark warriors would be landing at dual points along the coast—near Branth and northern Tsir'illia. From there, he would march east to take on the dwarves of Lorant once the people of Branthian were subjugated to his will and rule. With any luck, the main cities of Lorant would join him and together wipe out any resistance.

"Is it something we can help with?" Ril asked, eagerness tinting his voice as he lifted his head slightly.

"Actually, it is," Raer'dreth admitted, patting them both on the head like puppy dogs as he passed. "I will need every bit of energy from both of you to accomplish this, as the spell is going to be targeting more than a few bodies this time."

"Bodies? In the Endless Wastes, my Lord?" Xil asked, never lifting his head from the floor.

The archmage smiled. "Yes. The Wasting War claimed thousands of souls, both on our side and the humans." Raer'dreth bade the twins to stand finally and brushed some dust off their shoulders. "I'm going to be casting a wide-reaching spell that keeps bringing the dead back to life to do my bidding."

"So, they'll keep getting back up?" Xil asked, more than a little horrified.

"Until they are dismembered and only fragments, yes. Now fetch me the summoning bowl and bring a slave to sacrifice," Raer'dreth said with a note of finality that suggested—rather strongly—that the time for questions was over. "I have to scry and see if there is a body in Lorant I can use to bring Callen Drah back immediately."

Raer'dreth watched them run off, thankful the situation was salvageable, as he sat on his throne once more. *I'm out of wine,* he lamented to himself as he closed his eyes. He had to rethink his timetable now, but at least he wasn't caught flatfooted. His ships would arrive on the shores of Alian'tir in the next couple of tendays or so, then he would see what else he needed to do. *No matter. In another tenday, the Dark War will begin in earnest, and my enemies will tremble.*

Fort Kaldrin, Kingdom of Branthian

Alant and company rested at the knights' fort for the evening and prepared to ride out the next morning for the Capital with a knightly escort. Once Knight-Captain Marveth had let them off the hook, Syn'ella had become a welcome member of the party and warmed a few hearts among the knighthood, much to the displeasure of the Knight-Captain. The next morning, as the golden sun started to peek up from its long sleep, a few of the knights even went so far as to ask her about her sword skills and marveled at how well she used the small weapon. They cheered and watched in wonder as she twirled the sword in the air, laughing and dancing on the wind with her gossamer wings.

Everyone seemed enthralled with the faerie warrior—everyone except the second in command, Knight-Commander Feskar. "Is that even a real weapon, little warrior?" the man asked with a frown on his weathered face. His short black hair was slicked back, and his grey eyes seemed tired.

The tiny warrior spun her blade and flew over to him. "I hold the badge of a Warrior of the Ninth Thorn and have earned my slim sword by valiancy in action," Syn'ella answered, a growing smile on her tiny lips. "Am I to presume you are openly challenging me, Sir Knight?" The gathered host of knights held their breath, knowing that the Knight-Commander was known for his temper.

The man glowered, yet held himself in check, his fists shaking at his side. He took a deep breath and let it out slowly, finally looking at the faerie with a forced smile. "It is against the code to draw one's weapon against a helpless opponent," Knight-Commander Feskar countered, then turned on his heel and walked away.

The knights gathered around the faerie, offering their apologies, and it warmed Alant's heart to see the men who had once bullied him treat his friend with kindness. He was grateful that they were showing her respect and forgot all of his former prejudices against the knights who had teased him for years. Yet something else pulled at his chest as he looked over at the diminutive warrior, her wings fluttering out behind her. Syn'ella was *beautiful*.

Maybe it had been the frantic chase—and the near-death encounters—but Alant had never truly taken the opportunity to behold the faerie in depth. Her stunning figure, albeit tiny, was that of a full woman, and her golden hair fell upon bare shoulders. Her clothes were scarce—lightly armored means speed and agility on the field of battle—and she filled them out perfectly in every way. Alant looked away as he felt himself blush, yet his heart was pounding in his chest as he thought of her; a deep need to protect and cherish her was building inside him. She may only be two feet and some inches tall, but she made his pulse race all the same.

"Stories are full of the beauty of faeries, you know," Hylana said as she came up behind Alant. "There is no shame in looking."

Alant turned with a start and looked down at his feet. "I was..."

"You are young and she is very pretty, Alant. Hells, even *I* think she is gorgeous," Hylana admitted with a wink. "Now, let's go see about the supplies. I hear they are almost ready to leave."

Alant watched the sorceress go and thought about what she said. He had seen pretty girls before, and though he knew what he had felt back then, this seemed very different to him—like she was air and he needed to breathe...like she was water and he was dying of thirst. *Snap out of it, squire*, he berated himself. *Now is not the time to be dallying with these thoughts.*

The group rode out as the sun broke free of the distant horizon, an escort of only ten knights this time compared to the train of fifty that met them in the north. The refugees were still in the wagons behind them, fed and warm after a night's rest at the fort. Syn'ella rode with Hylana, talking to the sorceress about the faeries and the forest villages, and, of course, the magic of the elves. As they traveled through the morning, talk among the knights was light, and Alant reflected more on this feeling towards Syn'ella. Could he just be feeling like this because she had saved him? He watched her bounce slightly on the back of Hylana's horse and smiled. She was truly courageous for one so small.

"Smoke on the horizon, Knight-Captain," the lead knight called back.

Knight-Captain Marveth called for a halt and rode to the fore to see for himself. Hylana and Syn'ella rode up with him.

"What could it be, Knight-Captain? Hylana asked

"I'm not sure, but the village of Calian lies in that direction, maybe some twenty miles," Marveth answered.

"Should the knights ride and check it out?" Alant asked, concern edging into his voice despite his restraint. He couldn't take his eyes off that black smoke, knowing what it had meant in both Aran'tel and Faerin. *He's dead, though...*

"I'm sure it's just a farmer burning some branches or something," Marveth said, looking at Alant with narrowed eyes. A squire never second-guessed those in command. He turned and rode back, dismissing the smoke out of hand.

Alant sighed as they rode south, always keeping an eye on the smoke. It wasn't more than an hour later that they saw figures staggering toward them, calling for help. "Knight-Captain?"

"Hold formation and let them come, but be ready," The Knight-Captain said, his eyes narrowed. "It may well be a trap."

Alant could see the figures staggering and knew in his gut that they needed help. It didn't appear to be an act. The young squire kicked his horse out of formation and sped towards the figures just as they came into view; they were villagers and seemed beyond exhaustion.

"I gave no order to any knight to break formation!" Marveth called, fuming at the blatant disregard for orders.

"Well, it's a good thing Alant isn't a knight," Syn'ella said as she flew by the Knight-Captain, drawing her tiny, slim sword.

"Does no one listen to orders anymore?" Marveth asked the two knights next to him, but Hylana rode her horse up to him.

"Knight-Captain, even I can see that there are folk of the realm in need and that young man is riding to provide the exact service you swore an oath to do." The sorceress rode as well, galloping after Alant and Syn'ella.

"Weapons out and follow," Knight-Captain Marveth ordered as the ten knights with him turned and rode as one.

Alant reached the people and dismounted, offering help to an old farmer who was limping on a bloody leg. "What happened?" Alant asked, worried at the fear in the people's faces. *It can't be Samor, can it?*

"The dead..." the old man said as he collapsed in Alant's arms, exhausted.

Another woman came over and shook Alant's shoulder as if to urge him to listen. "You have to run, they're still coming. They don't tire at all!"

"Alant!" Syn'ella cried out, pointing to the west. The villagers were so out of it that they didn't even register that she was a faerie.

Alant looked and saw a group of men coming towards them. They were staggering awkwardly with weapons in hand. They wore no colors or emblems...in fact, they had barely any clothes on at all. Alant stood and stared in horror at what he was seeing, rubbing his eyes as if he were imagining the whole thing.

"They can't be what I think they are...can they?" Syn'ella asked as she hovered next to him, her wings beating like a hummingbird.

"I'm afraid they are," Hylana said, riding up to the two heroes. "It seems that someone had raised the dead of the wastes, and that means we are up to our eyes in trouble."

Alant couldn't believe it...Yet here they were, right in front of him and still coming strong. The bodies were all but skeletons, with scraps of clothes hanging off them. Their empty eye sockets had dirt and sand still pouring out of them, and rusty swords clung to skinless hands. They made no taunts or jests as they came, just an eerie silence to their measured, awkward steps and the occasional clacking of bone on bone.

"They only number at least twelve," Alant said, drawing Ilen'dar. The sword of light made a clarion call of hope once more, echoing across the plains. An answering horn came from the knights riding hard to them now, and goose flesh crawled up Alant's arm at the sound.

"These in front of you number that, yes," Hylana said, her eyes staring into the distance. "However, there are countless thousands buried under these sands from the Wasting War, young one." Worry edged into her voice as she turned to look at Alant. "Look. More come now, behind these." The sorceress pointed, and indeed another large group could be seen in the shadows of the high sun above, this group numbering close to fifty strong at least.

"They are no doubt on their way to Branth," Marveth said, coming up to them as his knights veered south to confront the dead. "We'll stop them here and hold the line."

"Captain, don't be foolish. Your men can't hope to hold out against so many," the sorceress said.

"I know that, lady. That is why Alant is going to ride—like the Goddess of Death herself is after him—back to Fort Kaldrin for reinforcements."

"No." Syn'ella's lyrical voice echoed in the stunned silence of the impending clash, her stern tone like water over the falls.

Alant turned to her, an inquisitive look on his face. "What's the matter, Syn'ella?"

"You are needed here...that sword is needed to fight the darkness that is coming," Syn'ella said, drawing herself up and turning towards Knight-Captain Marveth. "I hold the badge of a Warrior of the Ninth Thorn and have earned my slim sword by valiancy in action, yet I know that against these creatures, my worth is less than Alant's. I will go in his stead to Fort Kaldrin."

“My knights won’t listen to...” Marveth started to say, yet the tiny faerie drew her weapon and pointed it at him, her face a stern mask of challenge.

“I will take Alant’s horse and bring you your reinforcements on my life. If you do not believe me, then draw your weapon now, good Sir, and fight me,” Syn’ella said, not backing down from his malevolent stare.

It took three long moments, but finally, the Knight-Captain laughed, breaking the tension. “By Gar’heth, you *do* have some fire in you.” He waved her away as he drew his blade. “Why the horse, though? You have wings, surely you can fly.”

“Brave knight, the distance is far too great to fly fast and the horse will bear me swiftly,” Syn’ella replied, with a smile.

“Well said.” The Knight-Captain turned and faced the oncoming dead, his knights just starting to engage the first line of the walking dead. “Travel swiftly then, and know that you have won my respect this day.” He turned to the wagon driver and pointed to the south. “Ride for the Capital and don’t look back, we will follow when we can.”

Alant watched the old knight kick his horse and follow after his knights and smiled. “Hurry, Syn’ella, we’ll hold here while we can.” Alant felt a pang of fear at being parted from her—almost like he was afraid it would physically hurt—and was shocked to see her start to tremble as well.

“I won’t let you down, Alant,” Syn’ella swore, “Besides, I fear there is something we need to discuss upon my return. I feel a bond forming between us, Alant. I feel it is drawing us together, and I dread to be parted from your side. Keep safe until my return.” With those final words, she was gone, flying up onto his horse and riding quickly across the plains.

Hylana laughed as the faerie flew off. "Our lives are in the tiny hands of a faerie that, up until the last couple of days, I would have sworn on my soul was a myth."

"Don't you just love irony?" Alant asked as he watched the faerie speed off into the distance. Indeed, he had felt the link between them as well. It gave him hope for the future and instilled a desire to see her return. Alant raised Ilen'dar and rode forth to battle the dead.

Capital City of Llor, Kingdom of Lorant

Callen Drah was back, and she wasn't pleased at all. This new body was still reforming to her figure, and her armor was likewise building itself on her skin. She wasn't sure where she was, but wherever it was, the streets were rather clean. She had awoken in an alley, a knife in her chest, with no one in sight; it was always like this. When their souls were thrust back into the world, it was always either a prepared body or a recently dead body, though she had heard whispers of others being forced into the long departed with horrifying side effects. Callen shuddered at the thought and tried to focus on her surroundings instead.

Stone buildings stood all around her, with cobblestone streets and a warm air that came in from the south. The people all looked stern and hard-worked as she ventured out into the main fairway. Guards all stood at various intersections, giving everyone the hard eye as they passed. From what her master had told her about the area she was going to, this had to be Llor, the capital of Lorant.

Raer'dreth had told her that Llor was the seat of the king and his foul-tempered family. Nobles that made up the court of King Albron Brenshin were all backstabbing gossipers who wanted nothing to do with helping the people. The young king—who had succeeded his father near the end of the Brenshin War—wanted nothing to do with the nobles, but couldn't legally ignore them. Such was the state of Lorant, with ever-worsening politics and suffering for the common people.

Callen sighed as the last of her armor formed over her face and her sword reformed in its sheath, her long copper hair growing quickly out of the helm and over her shoulders. The suffering of the common people under nobles was why she hated kings and governments. She had sided with Raer'dreth, all those centuries ago, to be rid of things like this; people deserved to live free. Ironically, that was something she would never be. She strode out into the main street and was immediately hailed.

"You there, knight," a haughty voice called out as it rode past on a magnificent steed. Four lowly dressed men held the reins of the beast as they led it down the street, with one of them fanning the noble with a huge wooden slate.

"I am no ordinary knight..." Callen started, but the oblivious fool cut her off.

"I don't care who you are...you are in my way!"

Callen Drah stepped to the side and, as the man rode by, drew her shadowy blade and severed his leg at the knee with one swipe. As he fell screaming to the cobblestones, she walked over calmly and stuck her Shadowblade directly into his groin. "Listen to me, dog. You won't bother anyone ever again," Callen said over his constant screams of agony as she willed the magic of the sword to send hot ash coursing over his body. It issued from the blade as if crawling slowly out of slumber, burning and searing its way up towards his torso. The Knight of Shad'ar sheathed her blade and nodded to the four men who were frozen in terror, then turned to the burning body at her feet. His eyes were already turning black, and a black rot was spreading quickly as the ash burned his skin away. "Give my regards to Shar'in when you see her."

"Hold fast!" a guard called out, his voice shaking despite the steady hand that held the crossbow pointed at her.

Callen thought for a moment and smiled to herself. She knew exactly how to stop that elf girl from signing a treaty with Lorant and gaining allies against her master. She sheathed her blade and looked the man straight in the eye, her twin orbs flickering like a candle flame. "Take me to your king, then, guard, and I will explain myself to him."

CHAPTER EIGHT — PIECES ON THE BOARD

Fort Kaldrin, Kingdom of Branthian

Syn'ella saw the closed gates of the fort and knew there wasn't time for them to open them. Standing up on the running horse, she launched herself into the air and flew up and over the walls, calling out as she did. "To arms, Knights of the Realm!" she cried, landing in the grass and startling the watch knights on duty. The sun had just dipped down below the horizon, and she knew they were pressed for time.

"What is the meaning of this?" the stern voice of Knight-Commander Feskar bellowed as he came out of the main building. He was still dressed in his armor, like he lived in it. His cloak flew behind him with the evening breeze, his face looking like he would erupt into violence any second.

Syn'ella knew the man would never listen to her—in truth, she was hoping he wouldn't be awake when she arrived—but she had thought long and hard during the ride here and knew what she had to do; it was the only way. "We need the forces of the fort to assemble and ride within the hour—or sooner—Knight Commander, the lives of your fellow knights depend on it."

"What nonsense do you speak?" the man asked incredulously as he strode towards her. He pushed the watch knights out of his way and bore down on the faerie with a scowl. "You cannot barge in here and..."

"I challenge you to a duel, good and honorable knight," Syn'ella interrupted as she flew into his face and slapped him. The sound echoed across the yard as the knights gathered and held their breath in anticipation. "If I score a hit on you and draw blood, I will assume command of the forces at the fort.

Knight-Commander Feskar was furious and shook with barely constrained rage, his grey eyes closing as he tried to calm down. He drew his two-handed sword and gripped it in his armored hands, almost growling. "Only another knight may challenge his fellows to a duel," the man said.

"I am a Warrior of the Ninth Thorn, and as such, I am the equivalent of a knight in my realm," Syn'ella said confidently.

"So be it, faerie. I, Galbert Feskar, Knight-Commander of Fort Kaldrin, herby accept first blood, yet if I win, you will be locked in irons," Feskar said as he advanced.

Syn'ella swung her slim sword in the air for a couple of passes, as if testing the weight, and smiled. "Accepted—and may the best warrior win." Syn'ella wasted no more time, flying at the knight and swiping hard at his face. Predictably, he backed up as he couldn't get the large sword in line quickly enough.

He set his feet and swung in an arc that whistled through the air towards her, narrowly missing her wings as she dipped low. The gathered knights were dead silent, not even whispering to each other, so entranced they were at the fight. Knight-Commander Feskar sidestepped and swung again, almost impossibly quick with a sword so large, and found only air as his target yet again. "Stand and fight!" he yelled.

"I am fighting, brave knight." Syn'ella dipped again and flew between the knight's legs, coming up high and stabbing out with her slim sword at his shoulder plates. The tiny blade slipped through and found flesh, sinking deep as the knight cried out in shock and pain. The faerie warrior twisted the blade free, splashing drops of blood all over his cloak and the badge of office sewn on it. Syn'ella flew up, saluting the man as more blood seeped out of the crease of the metal. "First blood has been drawn!" she cried to the gathered knights. "I hereby assume command of the Kaldrin Fort and order all assembled knights to prepare to ride in defense of the realm!"

Knight-Commander Feskar growled louder and raised his blade once more, his grip on the blade so tight his armored gauntlets creaked. "You will..." he stopped when a knight stepped between the two and held up his hand.

"Knight-Commander Feskar, you have been struck and first blood has been drawn," the young knight said, smiling despite the commander's rage.

Syn'ella recognized him as one of the knights who talked to her when she first arrived and nodded her thanks when he looked back at her. "Do you yield to the duel, Knight Commander, and concede to the terms you agreed upon?"

"Very well, faerie, I concede to the duel and your terms," Knight-Commander Feskar said, still angry. He scowled at Syn'ella and bowed, albeit slightly. "Now, what is it you need the entire fort for?"

Syn'ella flew up so that all gathered could see her. "Your Knight-Captain and the others are fighting a horde of the dead that seeks to waylay the folk of the realm. They hold for the moment, yet will surely fall in the face of this evil without you. Though it is already dark, I implore you to ride." She flew up higher, her tiny voice echoing in the stunned silence of the gathered knights. "Ride with me to save them. Ride with me to save the realm they defend with their lives as we speak. I will explain in detail as we ride, but I say to you now...their lives depend on your haste this night." Syn'ella came down and looked at the Knight-Commander as the gathered knights cheered and went to rouse the others. She bowed to him and went to find Alant's horse. *I'm coming, Alant...I just hope it will be in time.*

The Capital City of Llor, Kingdom of Lorant

Falgrim knew something was wrong as she walked along the street, but she couldn't put a name to it. The ominous feeling was crawling up her spine with cold fingers and just wouldn't let go. They had arrived at the Capital city of Llor and were let right through the gates without hesitation. No questions, no harassment—just pleasant smiles and a welcome to the city; this was not the Llor she remembered at all.

"Lighten up, Falgrim, not everyone hates dwarves, you know," Anatarn said, clapping her on her shoulder.

"You aren't a dwarf," Falgrim replied and immediately regretted it when he frowned. Anatarn had married and loved a dwarf, so he knew their plight intimately. It was well known that any human who had even sided with the dwarves, much less married one, had been reviled by most of Lorant. *Maybe that's why I can't get him out of my head*, Falgrim thought as she scanned the streets ahead of them. *Why can't I stop this pull towards him?*

"They should've at least asked about my queen and the fact that I'm an elf," Eliyan said, her lyrical voice sounding troubled as well. "I had a speech prepared and everything."

Falgrim knew the elf had a point and was going to agree with her when two men up ahead drew her attention. They were leaning against a wall in an alley, but their weapons were out behind their backs, almost out of sight—almost. She casually flipped the catch on her baldric, fingering her axe. "Anatarn, remember how I fought Malakath?"

"Who could forget that," Anatarn said with a hearty laugh. "You charged him before he even knew what was going on." As if a torch was lit in his mind, a slow realization dawned across his face. "Oh, crap."

With a yell, Falgrim rushed the two men who were only twenty feet away at this point. Both men looked at the dwarven warrior with startled gasps, unprepared for the onslaught she was bringing to them, even though they were lying in wait. Hired thugs were used to being in charge, and catching them off guard was the best plan when dealing with them. Her axe whistled through the air and slammed into the first man's thigh, crippling him instantly as he fell screaming, his leg almost severed cleanly. He scrambled backward, crying for help as the blood poured out of him and into the street.

Falgrim lowered her shoulder into the second man and knocked the wind out of his body and into the mountains, hearing at least two ribs crack under the powerful dwarf's weight as she pinned him to the brick wall. Her knee came up into his head as he bent over, snapping his nose and sending him crumpling to the ground in a ball of cries and blood.

"Now!" came the call from six other men as they exited storefronts and side streets.

"Come on!" Falgrim shouted to her companions, picking up the fallen man's club and throwing it at the first man in range with deadly accuracy. The club slammed into the man's chest, spinning him as Falgrim grabbed her axe, yanking it out of the man's leg as his eyes fluttered, then shut as he bled out on the cobblestone street. "To the south gate!" Falgrim took off, pushing screaming people out of the way as the others came behind her.

Anatarn followed, keeping Eliyan and her friends in front of him as Falgrim cleared their path with brutal efficiency.

Falgrim noticed that the men were hanging back, either being cautious or... "They're funneling us; be ready," she cried behind her to Anatarn as she rushed past more people. The strange lack of a guard presence told her that wherever they were being herded to, it was going to be a bloodbath.

So be it, she thought. *Their funeral.*

Falgrim burst into a square devoid of people and skidded to a stop. Before her was Callen Drah, in her full armor, like nothing had ever happened. Around her, lying on the bloody cobblestones, were dozens of people, all nobles from what Falgrim could tell. It was difficult as there weren't many bodies left intact, though the house emblems spoke of high class.

"At last, there you are. I've been waiting for hours to see you again, dear dwarf," the shadowknight said as she slashed the air in front of her with the shadowy blade. "I've taken care of the king's noble problem, and in return, he has given you to me and forsworn any alliance with Tsir'illia. Now we get to see..." The axe slammed squarely into Callen's shoulder, burying itself deep—again—this time from the front.

Falgrim was already running at the dark knight, but knew that this time it was going to be different; that bitch had been waiting for them. Before she could reach the creature and retrieve her axe, Anatarn bolted past her, his dark blade in his steady hands.

"My turn," the warrior in black said as he rushed the dark knight.

Callen ripped the axe from her shoulder without a sound, throwing it far behind her as she faced Anatarn squarely. "You have no chance, no blade may wound me in hand-to-hand combat," Callen said, swinging her blade with the skill of her long years and stopping his charge cold. She attacked with ferocity and backed Anatarn up step by step. As they fought, small tendrils of ash leaked out from her blade and snaked through the air, their crackling sparks telling anyone who could see them that it was dark magic indeed.

Anatarn parried and spun, slicing the tendrils of ash and dissipating them with his blade as he backed away from her deadly sword. Anatarn was starting to sweat with the effort, and when he spun again—this time around her blind side—he narrowly avoided her upward slash.

"I know not how you dispelled my magic, but you can't make my sword disappear so easily, fool," Callen said as she pressed the attack once more. Her blade slashed up, missing him by a hair's breadth and taking his hat clean off.

Anatarn saw his opening. He stepped inside of her reach and sliced across her chest plate, the dark blade biting deep into the shadowy armor of the knight, as she had both arms raised, and came clean through like it had cut parchment. Dark shadows sprayed across the cobblestones, mixing with the human blood as Callen Drah howled from pain and shock, clutching the wound with one hand as she backed up in absolute horror.

"How?" she cried, clutching her chest as she staggered back. "Only Dark may wound me..."

“’Tis an elven blade of legend, dear creature,” Eliyan said, moving her hands together and pointing at the knight. Dozens of cobblestones ripped up from the street and hurtled at the Shadowknight. Callen’s sword deflected most of them, but some slipped by, knocking her further backward as they pelted her helm and shoulders. “The runes engraved upon its black blade give its elven name as Dar’kir or Dark.”

Seeing their chance, Falgrim ran by and grabbed her axe, tugging Anatarn’s arm. “Flee! We will live to fight another day,” she said. Knowing that he had to be tiring but wouldn’t want to run, she added something that would make him hear her. “I *need* you, Anatarn, *please*.”

Anatarn held his ground for but a second; then, as if her words broke through, he stared at her, relinquishing his stance. “Aye, all right.” He ushered Eliyan and her friends ahead of him and gave the dark knight one last salute as she dropped to one knee, the shadows spilling out of her wound.

Once they were almost at the gate, Falgrim slowed, taking a couple of breaths before they kept going. The gate was sure to be guarded. “Once we’re out of the city, we’ll make for the southern bridge to Llar. It’s one of the only larger dwarven cities outside of the Starsky Mountains, and I have friends there,” she said as they gathered around her.

Ongril shook his head and stepped back. “You go and take Eliyan. We’ll stay here and try to talk to King Albron.”

“You’ll most certainly be killed,” Eliyan said, tearing up. “I can’t let that happen.”

Ongril smiled warmly, laying a hand on her arm. “Look, Eliyan, you are a wizard and these two are warriors—some of the best I’ve seen even among our elves, mind you—but we’re just servants.” He turned to the others, and they all nodded. “If we go, we will just hinder your flight. If we stay, I may be able to convince the king of his error. Besides, that creature is most certainly coming after you." He smiled weakly at his lady and kissed Eliyan on the hand before turning to Falgrim.

"I know," Falgrim interrupted before he could speak. "I'll take care of her." The three of them left and headed for the southern gate, surprised to see it standing empty of guards. They sped out and across the bridge as horns blared, alerting them that the guard was coming. They wouldn't pursue past the city gates, but they all knew that the Shadowknight was going to be right behind them very soon.

Fields west of Calian, Kingdom of Branthian

Alant swung Ilen'dar with tired arms, doing some damage but not dropping the foul creature. They had been fighting for most of the day and into the night, and the dead didn't tire at all. The knights had lost more than a third of their number already, their weapons doing almost nothing to the bones of the skeleton warriors. With no vital organs to wound or pain to inflict, their only chance was to incapacitate them; that was more easily said than done in a full-fledged battle. The horses fell first, forcing the knights to fight on the ground and try to keep the dead from breaking through. Hylana threw spells at the dead with better effect, but had to switch to healing once the knights started falling. Thankfully, the moon had lent them enough light on the bloody plains to see their enemies clearly, but they were still at a disadvantage in the gloom; the dead had no such hindrances.

"Stand fast, men!" Knight-Captain Marveth called out, his sword ringing against bone with every hit. He had managed to take a dozen wounds and stay on his feet, being the beacon of hope in the battle; still, the knights rallied around Alant.

The knights called out Alant's name as he dropped another creature, Ilen'dar ringing out for all to hear with every creature slain. His skill impressed them, as he wasn't a knight, and more than once he saved another from an attack that may well have been fatal.

"She's not coming, is she?" one of the younger knights asked, fear emanating from his every word as he parried and struck at the ever-pressing enemy around them.

Alant smiled at the young man—Noral Percen, if he remembered correctly—as he parried a curved sword from one of the dead. He had been a year ahead of Alant and had already made knighthood. "Of course she is, Knight Percen. Syn'ella is a Warrior of the Ninth Thorn," Alant said, using her title as some kind of example that the man could use. He saw the knight nod his head, confidence filling his face once more. *If only I knew what a Warrior of the Ninth Thorn was, I would feel better, too.*

They fought and fell back, pressed and gave way, the dead just walking on towards them relentlessly, regardless of the fallen bones around them. Marveth took a curved sword through the leg, finally dropping, and another skeleton raised its weapon for the killing blow.

"Not today, old bones," Alant said as he ran in and parried the impending swing—denying them their kill—and stood over the fallen captain as a shield. "To me, men!" the young squire called out, his arms dropping slightly from exhaustion.

"Save yourself, boy," Knight-Captain Marveth said through clenched teeth. "I'm not walking on this leg anytime soon."

As if Alant knew what was on the man's mind, he looked over his shoulder at the Knight-Captain on the ground and smiled. "Syn'ella will be here, don't worry."

Another knight fell screaming, a wide-bladed sword in his helm turning that scream to a wet gurgle as it pierced deeper. As he fell, three more dead thrust their weapons through his armor and pinned him to the ground, his body twitching in its last moments. There were only four knights left now, besides Hylana and Alant, and the dead were pushing around them and on into Branthian despite their effort. The dawn was coming, yet the promise of a new day was clouded with blood and death.

Alant parried two swords and ducked a third as he swung again and again. His skill was fading with exhaustion, yet he would not fail.

"Leave me and stop them, Alant," Marveth begged. "You're the only one left to lead the knights." Before he could answer, a call went up in the impending dawn's light.

"She comes!" Percen called out, pointing back towards the east. "She comes!"

Thundering across the plains was a column of gleaming knights—at least fifty in number—with a tiny bright light at the fore. Syn'ella was on the lead horse, her slim sword catching the rising sun as she smiled at them. "Charge, Knights of the Realm, to battle!"

Alant gave a yell and swung Ilen'dar with renewed vigor. The charging knights fanned out and slammed into the dead like a tidal wave as the rays of the new day bathed the living and the dead alike. They pushed back the dead and kept the creatures from gaining any more ground, swords hacking and lances impaling the enemy with fervor.

“I told you to stay safe,” Syn’ella said to Alant as she flew to Alant’s group, her small sword glittering in the sunrise. The faerie warrior slashed and flew about in a circle, avoiding the strikes of the slower skeletons.

“I’m still in one piece, aren’t I?” Alant called over to her. He saw Percen go down with a scimitar in his leg and couldn’t get to the young knight in time. The dead bore down on him, but, at the last second, Syn’ella flew through them and knocked the dead over. While they were getting back up, she helped the young knight stand and smiled. “Legs...aim for the bottom bone.” Together, the two broke apart the dead around them as the knights crushed their enemies.

A cry went up as the last of the dead were broken and dropped by the knights. When it was all but over, Syn’ella flew to Alant’s side, slamming into him with the impact of a tiny horse. “Alant, thank Amara we got here in time,” she said, hugging him tightly.

Alant held her close, that spark coursing through them once again as they clung to each other. “Never leave my side again, brave Syn’ella,” Alant said as they finally broke apart.

“Never,” Syn’ella replied as she lay her head on his shoulder.

Soon, the survivors were being tended to by a weary Hylana as the knights finished off any of the dead still crawling. The sorceress was healing what she could, but there was a lot she couldn’t do. She, herself, had taken only minor wounds as her spells shielded most of the attacks, but she was exhausted from casting so much magic for so long.

“Shall we ride to the village and see what’s left?” Alant asked Knight-Captain Marveth as the man was getting his leg splinted.

"No, Alant." Hylana stepped in, concern on her face. She turned to the captain and shook her head. "We have to go, Knight-Captain. This was merely a small force sent to wipe out a village." She pointed back toward the Endless Wastes. "There are thousands of the dead out there, possibly already on their way—and not only towards Branthian."

Marveth held up a hand to forestall her. "I know, Hylana, I agree. We have to get back to the king and warn him, as well as settle the new bond we might be having with Tsir'illia before all hell breaks loose." This last was said with a smile towards Syn'ella. The Knight-Captain shifted his seat to better look at the diminutive faerie. "How *did* you convince my knights to ride for you, brave Syn'ella?"

A knight riding by stopped and saluted the Knight-Captain. "She flew in and challenged Knight-Commander Feskar directly. Syn'ella said if she scored a hit on him that drew blood, she would assume command of the forces at the fort. Knight-Commander Feskar was furious—of course—and accepted." The knight laughed as he spoke.

"I hit him on my second pass, clean through his shoulder plates," Syn'ella said, beaming with pride. "He conceded when the other knights called him on it."

"That I did, brave Syn'ella, Warrior of the Ninth Thorn," Knight-Commander Feskar said, walking up. The man was limping but whole and wearing a smile despite blood staining his black hair.

"Ah, Knight-Commander, I'm glad that you did, else we would be lost," Marveth said, clasping forearms with the man.

"I had my doubts, Knight-Captain," Feskar said, bowing to the faerie. "I had seen her when she arrived at the fort, and it seemed ridiculous that something so small could best a Knight of the Realm in combat. I am humbled in her presence."

"Thank you, Knight-Commander, but I only drew first blood. I needed to get you to listen to me quickly, and that was the only thing I could think of." Syn'ella turned to Alant as Feskar walked away. "We still need to talk, Alant, but for now let's get you some rest before we head out."

Alant nodded and looked around, seeing everyone working together. He knew now that the nations of Tsir'illia and Branthian would be able to come together; after all this, he was sure of it. He just had to convince the king. "I'll rest along the way; don't worry. It will be another three days to Branth, and we will have more of the dead coming behind us."

"But we'll have each other," Syn'ella said softly. "And once we're back in your Capital, we can have that talk. I want to relax with you on this journey and not worry about it till then, all right?"

"Sounds perfect to me," Alant agreed, then leaned on his horse as his legs went weak. "I may need a short nap soon anyway."

Castle Wrath, Isle of Raer'drin

Raer'dreth felt Callen Drah's pain as she lay bleeding shadows onto the ground. Another injury to one who was supposedly immune to attack. He curled his fingers in the workings of a spell and walked to his water pool. He wove the spell and spread his hands apart, the waters rippling with unseen magic. When the waters calmed, it turned into a sheer surface like a mirror, showing him the faraway realm of Llor. He could only do this easily with things he was connected to, like his Knights of Shad'ar.

The scene opened up, and he saw Callen, lying on her side in a marketplace, bloody bodies all around her as she healed slowly. Fleeing across the way was a dwarf, a human, and an elf working together in concert against him! He worked another spell and sent his voice across the ether. *Follow them, but do not engage again. I'm diverting a force of the dead to the east to assist you. Take them and scour whoever takes the heroes in. Destroy all who oppose you.*

Raer'dreth ended the spell and walked over to his map once more, looking at the city of Llor. They would flee south, possibly to Llar. He would send some of his dead through the Forest of Dust and hook up with Callen Drah. *Shar'in knows there are enough of them to spare*, Raer'dreth thought as he worked a spell of control. After that was done, he smiled and turned back to his current project—bringing back Samor Cah into another body after almost all of his life force was consumed in light.

Raer'dreth couldn't use the bodies he had here; they were already inhabited by the other knights, so he would have to gamble and let the soul find its own vessel somewhere in Alian'tir. This was the tricky part. Because he didn't have the soul of Samor under his control, he wouldn't be able to direct it to a fresh body. If the soul couldn't find one fresh enough, the magic might warp the soul and have dire consequences. *Serves him right for failing me,* the archmage thought bitterly.

CHAPTER NINE — STORIES TOLD

Plains south of Llor, Kingdom of Lorant

Anatarn looked behind them once more at the lone figure riding towards them. They had been traveling south for almost two days, and the Shadowknight had yet to close in on them; it helped that they were riding their horses near to death.

"It's still coming, isn't it?" Eliyan asked, fear tingeing her melodic voice.

"Yes, but for some reason, she's not catching up." Anatarn focused on the road ahead and looked to the horizon. Would anywhere they went be safe from this dark knight?

"I'm telling you; we should meet her on a field of our choosing and attack," Falgrim said, her irritation plain to anyone who had traveled with her for more than a minute.

"She's expecting us to do that, Falgrim," Anatarn said, convinced that the Shadowknight knew they would try to take her together. If that creature was still coming, then she was confident that she could win. He knew that his sword had hurt the dark knight, but it took everything he had to do that.

"But with both of us and your sword..." Falgrim said, then shook her head and dropped it. They had been over this for the entire ride and had agreed to get to Llar first.

Anatarn smiled despite the danger they were in. To see a dwarf drop something was like seeing a double rainbow...when it hadn't rained in weeks. The tension between them had grown, mostly because of how he was feeling for Falgrim. Anatarn had heard her say she needed him, and his heart stopped; Falgrim could not know that was what his wife had said before they had been separated in battle. *And I couldn't get to her in time,* he thought as he relived that horrific memory. Because of that, Anatarn had become distant, almost cold towards Falgrim, though he didn't mean to.

Falgrim called for a halt, dragging Anatarn out of his melancholic thoughts. A militia patrol from Llar was approaching with a husky dwarf in the lead. The southern reaches of Lorant were much more tolerant of the dwarves, as most of the fighting was done in the northern Starsky Mountains. Llar had prospered after the war, giving homes to the veterans who found scorn everywhere else. They created their own militia to patrol the land, saving the Red Warriors for the north.

"Hail the riders," the lead dwarf called out, motioning for his fellows to draw their weapons. He had a long brown beard, braided in three tails, and broad shoulders. Dark eyes sat under bushy eyebrows, and he carried a massive hammer that seemed too big for his short frame.

"Hail yourself, Jimson Stoutfist!" Falgrim called right back with a hearty bellow.

"Why, as I live and breathe, it's Falgrim Ironhaft," a stout dwarf female said as she put away her hammer. This dwarf had dirty blond hair and blue eyes, with a girth that compared to Falgrim's.

"Shut it, Belsa Harlow," Falgrim replied with a hearty laugh.

Anatarn welcomed the familiarity as he was worried that word of their flight might have reached the lower part of the nation by magic. King Albron may be distrustful of human sorcerers, but he still employed them, albeit sparingly. They could've sent word on the wisps of magic ahead of them, but it seemed that luck was on their side for once. "I take it you know these fine people, Falgrim?" he asked as they stopped.

"Jimson, this is Anatarn. Anatarn, this is Jimson, a fellow warrior and pain in the arse." Falgrim smiled as Jimson laughed. Falgrim looked over at Anatarn and winked. "Jimson and I go way back, before the war."

"Found yerself a human, Falgrim?" Belsa asked with more than a little sarcasm as she looked Anatarn up and down.

Falgrim actually blushed—and dwarves never did that. "He fought with the dwarves during the war, you old bag. He was at the stand at Brittleshan."

Jimson whistled and sat back on his pony, a look of respect on his bearded visage. "I heard about that. Lost a lot of good folk there."

"Does that mean he's free?" Belsa asked, her look turning more hungry than curious now as she stared at Anatarn.

"Shut it, Belsa!" Falgrim said with a huff.

Anatarn tried to smile, but the recent troubles had brought up too much pain, replaying that day over and over again. *Gods, how I miss you, Grinda*, he thought. He remembered what was chasing them and turned, expecting to see the dark silhouette of the Shadowknight in the distance, but there was nothing. She had been dogging them since Llor, but now it seemed she was gone. *Oh, that is not good*, he thought. *What could she be up to now?*

"I would love to trade war stories with you all, but right now there is something worse than that behind us," Anatarn said finally, nodding to Falgrim and Eliyan. "Let's get to Llar, and we can talk over a hefty pint of ale or five."

"Sounds good to me," Jimson said, turning to address his patrol. "Let's ride. If something is coming, I want Belsa and Falgrim in the rear. Move out!"

They rode quickly and, with only a few more miles to Llar, Anatarn was hopeful that they could at least get some rest before the hammer hit the anvil.

The Capital City of Branth, Kingdom of Branthian

Alant had never been more uncomfortable in his life. Knight-Captain Marveth had sent runners ahead of them to inform the king of the danger—and Alant's bravery—and it seemed that everyone now knew. He had always heard of court gossip but had never been the target of it before.

From the front gates of the grand city, all the way to the castle, the streets were lined with people cheering the knights and Alant. Girls threw flowers at him, and other women called his name with promises of being his wife. He was red in the face for at least six blocks in the city.

"Ignore them, Alant," Hylana said, riding next to him and Syn'ella. "This is what happens to heroes, and good-looking ones at that."

Alant shook his head and felt Syn'ella stiffen behind him. The faerie warrior had been awfully quiet since entering the city, and he supposed it was being among so many humans for the first time. In no time, they were at the castle, with knights keeping the people out and allowing the guards to escort them in.

Alant followed Knight-Captain Marveth with his small group through the corridors and into the main hall of Castle Branth amid stares and gossip. The body of Lord Knight Joran was carried behind them in honor and reverence, still wrapped in elven-scented cloth. As they passed, the other knights in attendance bowed and laid their swords on the floor, showing the fallen knight the deepest respect for valor in battle. The walk down the crimson carpet leading to the throne of the king went silent the minute Syn'ella was seen, the courtiers holding their breath at the sight of the faerie. For the first time in decades, they weren't even whispering to each other. Alant knelt at the base of the throne, head bowed in silence.

King Eldrian Danrae of Branthian sat on his throne, worry lines creasing his weathered face. He was in his late sixties with a full head of grey hair and deep blue eyes—eyes that had seen everything, at least until this day. His crimson robes, trimmed with golden thread, displayed the silver crest of Branthian on his chest—a silver sun with a sword. "Well come, Alant Landsir of Branth. Word of your bravery and valor in the recent attacks has reached this court, and we are anxious to hear the tale."

Knight-Captain Marveth went to one knee next to Alant, something that was *never* done. This move broke the trance of the nobles that lined the court's carpet, and the whispers started once more. One didn't lower oneself when they had rank. To kneel next to someone of lesser rank was admitting that they were your equal in all things.

"My King, the attacks are truly horrible. It gladdens my heart that my runners got to you ahead of us. Please allow me to take a legion out as soon as they are ready," Knight-Captain Marveth said with his head still bowed.

"Marveth, Alant, stand before me, please," King Danrae said with a voice soft yet compelling. He waited until they stood, then smiled. "I trust you both have *quite* a story to tell me, but you have the right of it, Knight-Captain," the king said. "It is imperative that the dead are stopped before they destroy any more villages. Take your legion in my name and fight well."

Marveth bowed and saluted, turning to Alant before leaving. "I hope to fight with you on the field again one day, Alant. May Gar'heth guide you." The Knight-Captain left and gathered knights to him as he walked down the carpet, leaving a very stunned gathering of courtiers behind.

Alant smiled, knowing that they would be shocked at a Knight addressing a squire in such a way, let alone a squire with a sword belted to his side. He turned his attention back to King Danrae and bowed his head once more.

The king waited until the doors were closed once more, then addressed Alant. "Now it is your turn, young squire. Tells us your tale, from the beginning, please."

"I will, my King. I also have proof of my words as well." Alant looked up and, with one hand held up in warning, he slowly drew Ilen'dar from its sheath. The courtiers all drew in a shocked breath, and the guards that were left drew their steel in response to this, yet Alant ignored them both. "This is the Light of the elves, named Ilen'dar, given freely to me according to the Silver Concordant." You could hear a faerie sniff in the silence that followed that statement, and it was a long pause indeed before King Danrae stood and cleared his throat.

"Clear the throne room," King Danrae said in a deep, compelling voice. The simple command hit the room like a falling dragon, the courtiers going pale and rushing towards the exit. The remaining knights sealed the doors behind them. Soon, the room only held Danrae, Alant, Hylana, and Syn'ella. "I have not heard that name in decades," King Danrae said as he stepped from his throne and descended to the floor to look Alant squarely in the eye. "My father, of course, schooled me in the prophecy before I took the crown, introducing me to the queen herself. However, I had not expected this to come in my reign." He eyed Alant with a smirk. "Why didn't Marveth tell the runners this as well?"

"I instructed him not to, sire. I wanted my words to come first," Alant said plainly. He had requested it of Marveth, and the Knight-Captain had agreed that it was his story to tell.

"Very well. Yet, can all this be true?" the king asked. "Things out of the darkest tales walking the land?"

Hylana bowed as she addressed the king. "Sire, if it helps, I was there when Squire Alant struck down the Shadowknight..." She was cut off before she could continue.

"So, it *was* a Shadowknight? Indeed?" Danrae paced now with his arms behind his back, lost in thought. "Times are truly upon us if Raer'dreth has finally sent his dark knights to this land. Tell me your story, young man, leave *nothing* out."

Alant told the entire tale, from the talks with Lord Knight Joran to the fight with Samor Cah; he left nothing out, except what he could not know...his arrival in Dyln'ir. What he couldn't tell, Syn'ella filled in, including her flight from this monstrous evil. They told the king about the dead and the charge of brave Syn'ella, as well as the plight of the village of Calian. Once they were done, the king stroked his chin and paced once more.

"So, Alant is not in trouble?" Syn'ella asked, flying up and bowing to the king.

The king just stared at the tiny faerie for a second and laughed. "No, brave Warrior of the Ninth Thorn, he is not. I believe your story. He has nothing to atone for in the eyes of Branthian. In fact, you both have saved us all if what you say about the dead is accurate."

"I fear to ask, yet I must, Sire. Will you honor the Concordant and bequeath the banner of Branthian?" Alant hated being forward, yet time was of the essence. He knew the queen was waiting, and the sooner they all joined forces against the dead, the better.

"A true man of action," the king said, his eyes gleaming in the fading light coming through the windows. "I find that your honesty, and indeed your resolve, leads me to agree with the elves on this. However, a *squire* cannot hope to wield such artifacts of power."

Alant's heart sank, his breathing shallow. He would fight anyway, even if it wasn't with this sword, or for this king; he would not fail his land. "I understand, my king. Then there is only one thing left to do," Alant said softly, reaching for his weapon belt.

"Quite right," Danrae said, drawing his sword in a flash. "That means I have to give you a title so you can wield them."

Alant was speechless as the king motioned him to his knees. Ilen'dar glowed with a pure radiance once more, this time giving off a warm aura of peace.

"Now, the only problem is what that vile knight had said...that no Knight of the Realm could hurt him." The king mused. "So, what should I call you?"

"Oh! I know!" Syn'ella shouted out, flying up close to the king in small circles. "Since he was named in the Silver Concordant, how about Silverlord?"

King Danrae nodded with a slight bow to the faerie and turned to Alant, his face growing serious. "Squire Alant, take this title and defend the realms of Branthian *and* Tsir'illia. No knight shall you be called; instead, you shall be Silverlord Landsir." King Danrae touched his blade to each shoulder, then sheathed his gleaming sword, clapping his hands twice. "Open the Court," the king said loudly.

The doors opened once more to the loud chatter of the nobles and courtiers outside, craning their necks to peek at what was happening. Another two claps brought two small boys, their shaggy hair in their eyes, as they bowed to the king. "Pages, please bring me the Banner of Branthian that rests in my quarters. Knights, escort the pages safely to me, let nothing and no one hinder them." They left and sealed the doors once more behind them as the nobles gathered around and whispered once more about what was happening. To see the king on the floor like this was unheard of.

Within minutes, the two pages were back, carrying a large black silk bag between them, the knights walking behind with hands on the hilts of their swords. The court went quiet once more as the silk bag was laid before the king, and as he sat back in his throne, he bade the pages to uncover it. Yet no banner did unfurl from the bag, but a shield of gleaming silver. It was a dark metal, etched with silver runes and the symbol of Branthian on the front—a silver sun with a sword. "Take up the Banner of Branthian, Silverlord Landsir, and wield it with honor in the name of our people."

Alant placed the shield upon his arm, feeling how light it was and the comfort it inspired. *The same as the armor the elves bequeathed me,* he thought. Before he could utter his thanks, a shimmering in the air appeared to their left—a portal slowly taking shape. The knights drew their weapons, and Alant drew Ilen'dar, the sword remaining quiet for once. They all let out a breath as Queen Tolandra of Tsir'illia walked through with Archmage Ereval upon her slender arm. Her wings unfurled and stunned the court.

"King Danrae," Ereval said, bowing low, his white hair draping across the crimson carpet. "I present to you..."

"I know who she is, good elf," the king interrupted, walking forward and kissing the queen's hand. "It appears we have a *lot* to talk about, dearest Tolandra."

Alant and Syn'ella moved aside as the king and queen talked, the knights removing the courtiers once more amid shouts and objections. "Time for that talk?" he asked as he ran his hand through her hair.

Syn'ella closed her eyes and flew up into his arms. "I don't know where to begin..."

"I think I do," Ereval said, walking up beside them. He laughed at their shock and smiled. "I'm an archmage, remember? I can see magic when it appears right in front of me, and the soulbond is rather strong between you two.

"The what?" Alant asked as his heart fluttered, and embarrassment clearly showed in his reddening cheeks.

"It's a special bond between two people," Syn'ella started, blushing a bit herself. "It means that they are destined to be with each other for the rest of their lives." She turned to Ereval and folded her tiny arms across her chest. "But I thought only elves and dwarves could have those—and it was rare to cross race?"

"A soulbond is rare to any race, but it can happen to anyone. It is extremely rare for faeries to enter into one with someone, but not unheard of," Ereval said, turning towards Queen Tolandra. "The queen's parents were an elven archmage and a faerie warrior."

"So that's what I've been feeling," Alant said, smiling down at Syn'ella. He was glad to know it wasn't just a fleeting feeling or raging hormones.

"I'm terribly sorry, Alant," Syn'ella said, looking down. "I know you must want a regular-sized girl of your own kind to be with." Syn'ella's eyes were filled with unshed silver tears, and she started to turn away, closing her eyes tightly. "There were so many girls out there who wanted you—and they were all prettier than me—that you could have your pick now that you're a hero and all."

Alant put both hands on Syn'ella's tiny waist and held her in place, turning her to face him. He lifted her to look her right in the eyes, despite them being shut. "What I want, brave Syn'ella, is a woman who will stand by my side no matter what and have the courage to risk her very life for me and others," he said, his voice soft yet serious. "You are the prettiest girl I have ever seen, and no one could compare to your inner beauty. Now open your eyes."

When Syn'ella opened them, her tears on the verge of falling, Alant kissed her. It was a tiny kiss on her perfect lips, but the spark that ignited between them was enough to draw attention from the rest of the room. Light flared out from them without sound, and even Ereval stepped back, shielding his eyes. Alant knew instinctively that they had both accepted the bond, feeling his soul mesh with hers like a puzzle piece. Her heartbeat was his now, strong and vibrant despite her size. "Never leave me, Syn'ella."

Syn'ella was crying now, those held-back silver tears flowing freely, yet with a smile that seemed like the sun itself. "As long as time moves forward, Alant, my sword and my heart will defend you," Syn'ella said with a passion most women could never muster. She kissed him again, this time deeply, as she held his face in her hands. When she pulled back, she smiled at him warmly, placing her hands on her hips. "Nice talk."

City of Llar, Kingdom of Lorant

Falgrim drained her mug again, slamming it down on the wooden table harder than she wanted to. They had found no trace of the dark knight and heard nothing from Llor about any of the famous Red Warriors coming for them. In fact, the Lord of Llar had heard nothing from his king in over a tenday.

"I don't like it," Anatarn said, finishing his drink. "It can't be over just like that."

"Why not?" Eliyan asked, sipping her elven wine. "That dark knight now knows that Dar'kir can wound her, and she did end the treaty between my land and Lorant. Maybe her work here is done?"

Anatarn looked up at the elf with a frown. "I never asked before, Eliyan, but how did you know the name of my sword? I've never noticed any runes on it," Anatarn said, drawing the blade slowly as the other patrons watched and laying it on the table.

"They would be hard to see with your normal human sight," Eliyan said, leaning over and tracing them with her finger. "Right here, there are tiny marks that seem to be imperfections leading up to the hilt; those are the runes."

"You mean these? I always assumed they were nicks or scratches on the steel," Anatarn said as he ran his hand over the blade gently. "I wonder how my grandfather came to own this sword?"

"As a wizard and a healer, I know a lot of the histories of our people, yet the mystery surrounding Dar'kir eludes me," Eliyan said, shaking her head. "I would have to ask Ereval Drial, the archmage in Dyln'ir. He is an expert on elven weapons through the ages."

"Naming weapons...another elven thing that irks me," Falgrim said as she held her arm up for another round.

"I'll go get them, Falgrim," Anatarn said with a slight smile. "Don't hit anybody while I'm gone."

"No promises."

Once Anatarn was a good thirty paces away, Eliyan slid her chair closer to Falgrim and leaned in, despite the dwarf's scowl. "He doesn't fancy me, you know," Eliyan said quietly so only Falgrim could hear.

"What're you going on about now?" Falgrim asked, looking down at the table as she shifted her seat away from the elf. The wizard had seen right through her and nailed the hammer right on the anvil; that made it even worse.

"It's plain to anyone traveling with you that you like each other, yet there seems to be something like a wall up..." Eliyan stopped as Falgrim looked up and eyed her coldly. "What?"

"His wife was killed in the war, and I think I remind him of her," Falgrim admitted, her ire fading as the truth came spilling out like water over the falls. Saying it out loud made it all the more real to her, and she felt defeated before she even began the fight.

"That's horrible, yet surely he likes you as well, it's all over his face when he talks to you," Eliyan said as she took a sip of wine.

Falgrim laid her head down on the table. This pretty little elf girl was the last person Falgrim would've ever talked to about anything, yet she couldn't stop for some reason. "He is all I can think about—when I'm not fighting that is—and I must bring back terrible memories of her," Falgrim said, raising her head and staring at the elf. "Those memories would eventually cause him to resent me, so it can never work out between us."

"You look nothing like her," Anatarn said, setting down Falgrim's drink and resting his hand on her shoulder, making her jump. He recalled his hand as a spark ran through it again, but he shook his hand and smiled down at her. "She was twice your girth."

Eliyan spat out her wine and laughed as Falgrim stared up at Anatarn with her mouth wide open. "How long have you been standing there?"

"Long enough." Anatarn sat down and looked at Falgrim, holding her rough, calloused hand. "I'm sorry if I've been cold these last few days, it's just what you said back in Llor..."

"I never should've said that..."

"No. It's just...that was what Grinda said before we got separated. We drifted apart in all the fighting, and then she was surrounded and needed me, but I was pinned down and couldn't get to her," Anatarn said, a tear falling slowly down his face. "I heard her keep calling to me as she died, saying my name over and over as they overwhelmed her. I killed every last one of them once I got free, but it didn't bring her back."

Falgrim knew right then that she was falling hard for this warrior. To a dwarf, regretting decisions in battle was like breathing. Admitting them to another showed that you deeply cared for whomever you shared those regrets with; it was why dwarves were always so tight-lipped about battles they fought in. Anatarn had to have known this. "You know a lot about dwarves, but there is one thing you missed," Falgrim said, taking a swig of her drink. "When a dwarf knows they are going to fall in battle, they either go down praising another dwarf's clan or repeat a loved one's name over and over as they pass, so that they carry the memory of them into the afterlife."

"That is so beautiful," Eliyan said, a tear falling down her cheek now as she listened intently.

"Thank you, Falgrim," Anatarn said softly. "I never knew that."

"Well, now you do. Don't worry, though, I'll never ask you to save me; I'm the better fighter anyway," Falgrim said with a smile as she punched his arm. Yet a deep fear twisted inside of her, a burning in her chest as she stared at him. Falgrim finally guessed what had happened with the spark she had felt in Halstrad whenever they touched. *Oh no... please, it can't be. Not with him,* she thought, trying to keep that fear out of her face. They were becoming Heartbonded.

To be heartbound to another in dwarven life meant they were destined to be together until the Great Hearth called them home. It was very rare, but it was in all the stories Falgrim had read as a young dwarf. She had read some stories about dwarves having it with other races, but they always ended in sorrow, mainly because of how long dwarves lived—at least twice that of a human.

Yet it seemed that they had survived, and with no enemies in sight, they could head west and seek out sanctuary in Branthian. *Maybe even head back up north the long way*, she thought. *Settle down in Halstrad.* For now, though, she had to figure out this bond and what she was going to do about it.

EPILOGUE — THE DARK RISES

Capital City of Branth, Kingdom of Branthian.

Over the next tenday, Alant witnessed the treaty rewritten to proclaim the nations of Tsir'illia and Branthian true allies. They would be sharing knowledge of the enemy from their oldest records, and the no-trespass was lifted. Alant was restless, though; he knew there was more to be done. It was a feeling deep in his gut more than anything else, a feeling that they needed more, even though everyone said the dark forces would be held back easily.

So it was that Alant found himself in front of King Danrae before the man was set to retire for the evening, the court whispering at the inconvenience of the hour. "My King, I have a request," Alant said, going to a knee and bowing his head.

King Danrae stood and shocked the court by laughing. "Silverlord Landsir, you do not have to bow and curtsy like a noble of this court. A simple inclination of respect is fine." The king walked down off the dais that the throne sat upon and clasped the young warrior on the shoulder. "What do you desire?"

Alant was uncomfortable with the familiarity the king was showing him of late; the knights had noticed it as well, but deigned to say nothing. As it was, the title he was given was spread to every outpost and fort by way of messenger so as to inform them if he ever traveled the land. Now it seemed that he could benefit from that. "King Danrae, I was hoping that you could grant me a leave so that I may travel to the nation of Lorant."

"War is already upon us, Silverlord Landsir. Do you have family there?" the king asked, curiosity blossoming in his eyes.

"No, my King. I was thinking that with our two nations working together to face the coming darkness, another aiding in that case would be even better." Alant held his breath after that. Lorant was known for two things. Mining the gold shards that all of Alian'tir used for currency, and being stubborn when dealing with anyone else.

"I think you are wasting your precious time, Silverlord, yet it would be good to have all nations working together." The king sent for his pages and sat back down on his throne. "Travel to Lorant and see what you can, but be careful... King Albron Brenshin is not as kind as I, nor as pretty as Tolandra. We will hold the darkness at bay until your return."

Alant smiled and bowed slightly, taking his leave.

"One more thing, Silverlord Landsir," the king said, causing the whispers that had started to cease immediately. "I hope you are taking Syn'ella with you."

By now, word had spread of the pair's coupling, and rumors had already flown through the castle. Alant had ignored them with practiced ease. "I planned on it, sire, but may I ask why you wish it so?" Alant wasn't sure what the king's reasons could be.

"Well, I want Lorant to know that we have treated with Tsir'illia, and you're traveling with a faerie will be good reinforcement of that truth." King Danrae chuckled a bit and then continued. "Besides, I want her to annoy Brenshin."

Alant laughed at that and nodded his head. "It will be done, My King. If it turns out they won't treat with me, perhaps I may find allies in that nation regardless."

"I've heard that factions of dwarves are unhappy with their treatment, though why none has ever ventured into Branthian is beyond me; perhaps you are correct. Safe travels, young lord, and hurry back. We need heroes such as you to battle Raer'dreth and whatever he may send at us," the king said as Alant inclined his head and then walked away.

Alant met with Syn'ella in his room and kissed her. "He is letting me travel," Alant said as they broke apart.

"Are we leaving right now? Or do we have time for some more fun?" Syn'ella said with a smirk.

Alant blushed and tried to smile. They hadn't had sex yet, but they did try a whole lot of other things, much to the young boy's surprise. He was shocked to learn Syn'ella's age and that she was so experienced. Neither of them was sure how it would work when they tried it, but for now, they were just experimenting while they relaxed. "We will leave in the next day or two, so yes, we can have fun."

"Oh, my heart," Syn'ella said, kissing him again. They didn't know how long they had in this life, and they were making the most of it while they could. They rode out of Branth soon after, heading east towards destiny.

Forest of Tsir, Northern Tsir'illia

He tried to scream as the pain wracked his very soul...but his mouth was full of dirt. He couldn't move or see, and the agony would not cease. He could feel his limbs strengthen with the excruciating waves of torture, and he tried to move them upwards; he hoped it was upwards at least.

Pushing the dirt with his preternatural strength caused more pain, as his joints ripped and tore due to the amount of pressure he was exerting. After agonizing hours of inching his way through the ground, his hand broke the pressure of his confining prison, and he felt air once more, although it felt much different than usual.

Samor Cah was back, yet he could feel that something was wrong, deeply wrong. Usually, when a Shadowknight came back, they could remember being in their crystals, awaiting dispersion to a new host body. That trip was soothing, almost euphoric, and once Raer'dreth called them, they floated up and soared to the new body where the magic would transform it to match their original look and dimensions. This time, however, he couldn't recall where he had been or the trip at all. The only thing he had felt was a grip, as cold as the death he usually gave to others, around his very soul, and then he was here. *Wherever here is*, he thought.

Likewise, this time he couldn't feel the changing of the body. Samor was a big man in life—easily over six and a half feet—and new bodies grew and shaped to fit that image. This time, he felt cramped, stuffed inside a body that wasn't changing to fit his tortured soul.

Samor broke more ground and finally lifted his dirt-caked face, waiting for the telltale red/orange tint to his vision afforded by the flames within. With those flaming eyes, he had been able to see almost anything nonmagical hidden from him, yet now his empty eyes saw only a green hollow tint. The Knight of Shad'ar crawled out of the hole in the ground, trying not to panic. He had heard nightmare stories of things like this from some of the other spirits when something went wrong, but he wasn't going to think about that yet. Standing up, he stretched and saw that his shadowy armor wasn't appearing either, nor was his sword of shadow at his side. He opened his mouth to scream and realized that air was blowing right through his mouth before he opened it.

Raising his hands to his face, he staggered in horror at the sight. His very hands were bleached bone! He touched his face and could not feel anything, his skeletal hands lacking feeling, yet the bare skull beneath was plain to their touch nonetheless. Samor Cah, feared Knight of Shad'ar, looked down upon his body and saw that he was a rotted corpse of a person, long forgotten in an unmarked grave.

"Amara's leaves!" a lyrical voice cried out. "What abomination is this?"

Samor turned to see two elves standing, arrayed in armor, their weapons out in shaking hands. They were alone, possibly a scouting patrol, and their eyes were wide with fear. "Where is this place?" Samor asked, hearing his own voice as a disembodied whisper more than the booming tenor he usually had.

"Back, foul creature of the dead!" The other elf said, making the sign of Amara.

“Your nature goddess won’t save you this time,” Samor said, striding towards them. He had no weapon, yet centuries of skill at arms gave him the confidence to take on double their number with his bare hands.

Realizing they had no other option, the two elves separated and circled the undead knight, trying to flank him. One had a large hammer, intricately carved and adorned with runes. The other had a slim sword, almost too short to do much of anything in a real fight.

“I ask you again, elves, where is this place?” Samor asked, trying to figure out where in Alian’tir he had arrived.

“You are in the northern part of the Forest of Tsir,” the first elf answered as he kept circling. “How is it that you were called from the grave and can speak, foul creature?”

“Tsir’illia? Now that *is* good news. Tell me, are we near the sea?” Samor couldn’t believe his luck. He could keep on his course of destroying the elves at least, though without his sword, it would be harder against their magic. The shadowy blades of the knights could turn some lesser magics aside.

“We will tell you nothing more, dead thing. We will send you back to the ground whence you came.” The second elf moved in with his slim sword, totally unprepared for the level of skill his opponent had.

Samor sidestepped at the last moment, almost losing his balance with his shorter body, and caught the elf around the throat with his bare skeletal hand. His strength had grown even more since standing out of the ground, and now he simply crushed the elf’s neck in his grip, shaking the body like a child’s doll. “Oh, you *will* tell me, one way or the other,” he promised as he faced the other elf with the hammer.

The elf’s courage broke, and he dropped his weapon as he fled into the woods. Samor quickly picked up the hammer and threw it with everything he had. His aim was true, catching the elf in the leg, shattering the bone, and dropping him in a tumble that sent him sprawling against a tree.

The Knight of Shad'ar stalked towards the elf as the lithe, helpless soul attempted to crawl away, his cries for help echoing amongst the trees. For the next hour, Samor took out his horror and anger on the elf, getting everything he needed to know before he died. His anger sated—for the time being—Samor Cah went back to the grave he came out of and dug up the area around it, looking for anything that may have been buried with the body he was in. He found a set of blackened, ravaged armor and laughed; this would do for now. Donning his new skin and hefting his acquired hammer, he set out west through the forest.

The elf had told him that a small elven town lay to the north—Illren, he called it. West of that, however, was the prize he was looking for—the Queen's tower itself. Samor Cah walked with purpose once more towards his destiny, and woe to anyone who stood in the dark knight's way.

Castle Wrath, Isle of Raer'drin.

His dark robe swirled around him as he walked down the stone corridor, his bare feet echoing in the empty hallway. Everyone had been called to the main courtyard to hear him speak, and not even the servants were exempt from this missive; the day he had been waiting for had finally come. The archmage Raer'dreth Iliad was a dark elf of the great house Iliad; the first, actually. Centuries ago, he had bargained with

Shar'in—Goddess of Death and Shadows—for the power of shadow magic so he could command the spirits of the dead. What the archmage had not anticipated was the magic turning his beautiful pale skin charcoal black. It was a small price to pay for the power it gave him, though.

"My Lord," one of his retainers started to say as he turned onto the open balcony. "You should..."

"Shut it, Dravon," Raer'dreth said, cutting the man off. He flipped his long white hair back so that his pointed ears showed clearly and stared out over the sea of people with calm, grey eyes. "I've been alive long enough to remember your grandmother. I think I know how to approach my people."

Draven simply bowed and moved out of the way quickly, lest he find himself falling towards the courtyard.

Raer'dreth twisted his two fingers in a spiral and used magic to amplify his steady voice. "People of Raer'drin, the day has come at long last to enact our vengeance upon the heathens of Alian'tir. Justice will be served for casting me out and replacing me with their false gods, and you will be my instruments in this holy war."

The crowd below surged with pride, their fists banging upon their chests with fervor and their voices drowning out his thoughts. It still amazed him that these people thought he was a fallen god when he arrived on this forsaken piece of land. The natives—over two hundred years ago—had deemed him their god and worshiped his power over the dead. He had cultivated their religious zeal all these years, and now they were an unstoppable force that would bring his war to the people who cast him out.

"Silence!" Raer'dreth commanded, and the crowd fell silent within a breath. "Now is the time, warriors of Raer'drin. Board the black ships and sail for the shores of our enemies." Raer'dreth ended in a gesture that called forth tendrils of shadow, blasting harmlessly into the air above them all, and the crowd roared once more. It would take the slow black ships almost a tenday to reach the shores of Alian'tir. Yet when they did, the Dark War would finally be upon them. *Then, I will bring pain and death to my enemies, and they will regret turning on me all those years ago*, he thought as he twirled around and walked back down the hallway. Yes, his plans were finally coming to fruition. Even the re-summoning of Samor Cah's essence, though flawed, could be used to his benefit. Now he needed some aged wine and a good slave to torture, and his day would be complete.

"Master," a familiar voice called out behind him.

Raer'dreth winced and closed his eyes; he was in too good a mood to be annoyed with his progeny this day. "What is it, Xil?"

Xil smiled as he came around, bowing low and never making eye contact with the powerful archmage. "Ril and I are ready to see the ships off, yet we were wondering if you wanted the people to witness our power or not."

Raer'dreth nodded and raised his hand to his chin. It was certainly a conundrum. Perhaps the time had come to reveal his progeny to the people. When they were first born, he had slain the mother outright and kept them a secret from the people of Raer'drin. If they knew he had conceived children, they might also worship them, and he did not know how that might play out; now, however, it might work in his favor.

Raer'dreth sighed with a small smile. "I see no other way around it, Xil. Tell your brother that he doesn't need his hood or gloves and to proudly show off his heritage when you cast your spell. I will be there to quell any whisperings."

Xil's blue eyes widened with shock, and his smile almost took over his entire face, though he looked away, trying to hide his enthusiasm. "I will, and we will bring greatness to House Iliad, don't worry...Father."

Raer'dreth watched him scurry away, almost skipping down the corridor. The twins would cast their prophetic spells to give the seventeen ships good fortune on the seas and favor the weather, as well as mask their own surprise that he had on each ship. He sighed, and a slight smile tugged at his mouth. Raer'dreth generally hated it when the twins called him Father, yet today it brought a faint smile to his dark lips. They irritated him—almost constantly—yet deep down, he did enjoy their presence. It wasn't a normal kind of affection, yet in his own way, he would miss them when they died. Half-elves never outlived their elven parents, especially one as strong in shadow magic as Raer'dreth. They would age more slowly than humans, living almost two, maybe three hundred years. Elves would see that twice over if not more. The archmage shrugged and continued on his way to procure wine and enjoy the rest of the day before the final send-off.

THE END OF BOOK I

APPENDIX - GLOSSARY

Albron Brenshin: King of Lorant and son of Alban Brenshin. Signed the treaty with the dwarves upon his father's death.

Alant Landsir: Young squire of Branthian under the tutelage of Lord Knight Joran. He is well over six feet tall with black hair and cinnamon eyes. Soulbonded to Syn'ella and wields the sword Ilen'dar, or Light as it's called in common.

Anatarn Blackblade: Human warrior from Parsil in the south of Lorant. He has long black hair and dark eyes, and dresses in black leather armor with a wide-brimmed hat. Wields the sword Dar'kir or Dark as it's known in common. Heartbonded to Falgrim Ironhaft

Amara: Goddess of nature and magic. Revered by the elves and faeries, this goddess is worshipped by anyone who casts magic and lives in nature.

Belsa Harlow: Female dwarf who's part of the standing militia. From the city of Llar in Lorant. Has dirty blond hair and blue eyes.

Bloodmage: Human sorcerers who have taken a darker turn. They use stones and words as well, but use blood as a catalyst to allow their spells to bypass wards and even armor, as it targets the very lifeblood of the enemy directly.

Branth: Capital city of Branthian and home to King Danrae's court. Fortified port city south of the King's Wood.
Branthian: Nation on the western coast of Alian'tir. Ruled by a democratic monarchy and protected by Knights of the Realm. Its capital is the fortified city of Branth.
Brenshin War: War between the dwarves of Xarvan Tor and Lorant over the rights of shard mining. A bloody conflict that saw the fall of King Alban Brenshin and started dwarven racism in Lorant.
Callen Drah: Female Knight of Shad'ar and undead warrior of Raer'dreth. She has long copper hair and twin pools of liquid fire for eyes. Known also as a Shadowknight from myth.
Code of the Knights: This huge book, located in the capital city of Branth, has thousands of pages detailing everything a Knight of the Realm would need to act with both honor and courage in everyday life. It is followed until death.
Dravon: Retainer to Raer'dreth Iliad.
Dyln'ir: Capital city of Tsir'illia and home to the largest school for magic in all of Tsir'illia. Lies in the south of the Forest of Tsir.
Eldrian Danrae: King of Branthian. Lives in the capital city of Branth. He has grey hair and deep blue eyes. His crimson robes, trimmed with golden thread, display the silver crest of Branthian on his chest—a silver sun with a sword.
Eliyan Safril: Female elven wizard/healer from the house Safril. She lives in the city of Ulin'or in Tsir'illia. She has long white hair and deep violet eyes. Niece to Queen Tolandra.
Endless Wastes: The wastes are a large section of parched desert in the center of Alian'tir. Created by foul magic during the ancient Wasting War between Branthian and Tsir'illia.
Ereval Drial: Archmage of Dyln'ir. He has flowing white hair down his back and piercing violet eyes. Wears a white silk robe

trimmed with gold and a cloak of diaphanous mesh. Soulbonded to Kysen Drial and an expert on history.

Falgrim Ironhaft: Dwarven female axe-for-hire. From the dwarven mining city of Xarvan Tor in the Starsky Mountains. Has thick hair done in three long, black braids hanging down her back. Short and well built. Heartbonded to Anatarn Blackblade

Galbert Feskar: Knight-Commander of Fort Kaldrin in Branthian. Has black hair and grey eyes. Second in command to Knight-Captain Marveth.

Gar'heth: God of honor and battle. He is worshiped by warriors and knights, as well as most dwarves. He is often called upon before battle.

Gnarr: Squat, filthy creatures with long matted hair and gray skin, covered in scars and warts. Their teeth are more often missing than not, and they have an appetite for just about anything.

Grinda Silversmith: Female dwarf who died during the Brenshin War. She was lost at the Stand of Brittleshan. Wife to Anatarn Blackblade.

Halin: Old man of Halstrad.

Heartbonded: See Soulbond

Hylana Brendal: Female sorceress of Branthian. She has long black hair and green eyes. One of the most powerful sorcerers in Branthian due to her fast thinking and improvising.

Jerix: God/Goddess of thieves and money. This god, perceived as both male and female at times, is worshipped by cutthroats and moneylenders as well as some dwarven miners.

Jimson Stoutfist: Male dwarven militia captain. Lives in Llar, in Lorant. He has brown hair, dark eyes, and a long brown beard, braided into three tails.

Knights of the Realm: Knights of Branthian who follow a strict code called the Code of the Knight. They dress in gleaming plate and fight with swords on horseback.
Kysen Drial: Lady of the capital city, Dyln'ir. She has long white hair entwined with violet flowers and deep amethyst eyes. Soulbonded to Ereval Drial and an accomplished wizard.
Llor: Capital city of Lorant and seat of trade for the east coast. Home of King Albron Brenshin's court. Trade port city southeast of the Starsky Mountains,
Lorant: Nation on the eastern coast of Alian'tir. Ruled by a hereditary monarchy and protected by the Red Warriors of Lorant. Its capital is the trade city of Llor.
Malakath Hiram: Human sorcerer and bloodmage in the northern town of Halstrad. He has pale skin, red hair, and his face is covered in freckles. Dresses in yellow and green and secretly works for Raer'dreth.
Marcus Joran: Lord Knight of the Realm in Branthian and expert in the Code of the Knight. He has short black hair that is graying on the sides and soft blue eyes.
Noral Percen: Knight of the Realm. He is stationed at Fort Kaldrin in Branthian.
Ongril Silvertree: Male elf and steward to Eliyan Safril. He is from Ulin'or in Tsir'illia. he has short white hair and emerald green eyes. Practiced in etiquette and the ways of most courts.
Raer'dreth Iliad: A dark elf of the great house Iliad and Ruler of Castle Wrath. He lives on the island of Raer'drin in Castle Wrath and has long white hair and grey eyes. Powerful Archmage.
Raer'drin: Island to the northwest of Alian'tir, populated by barbaric people who worship Raer'dreth as their god.

Red Warriors of Lorant: Warriors trained to serve the king of Lorant in all things until death. They wore gleaming chain and wielded long silver lances with plumes of red on their silver helms.

Ril Iliad: Half-dark elf and prophetic wizard. He lives on the Isle of Raer'drin in Castle Wrath. He has faded white hair and ice-blue eyes and has an identical twin, Xil.

Samor Cah: Male Knight of Shad'ar and undead warrior of Raer'dreth. He has raven black hair and twin pools of liquid fire for eyes. Known also as a Shadowknight from myth.

Sarin Marveth: Knight-Captain of the Knights of the Realm. He lives in Fort Kaldrin, also known as Knight's Rest in Branthian. He has grey hair and brown eyes.

Shadowknight: Creatures of myth and legend, these undead knights exist as souls that inhabit bodies that are recently slain. They rise and conform the body to their likeness and cannot be permanently slain by conventional weapons. Also known as Knights of Shad'ar.

Shar'in: Goddess of Death and Shadows. She is worshiped by murderers and malcontents as well as the Gnarr race, who call her Sar'in.

Shards: These tiny fragments of gold ore are mined by the dwarves for the rest of Lorant—the whole of Alian'tir. It is the standard currency of the continent.

Silver Concordant: Centuries-old treaty between Tsir'illia and Branthian. A clause or addendum states the following: 'When the knight of shadows falls to the sword of a boy, the elves must give him their Light, and the humans their banner; only then can the Landsir rise and protect us all.'

Sorcerer: Humans who use special stones to focus magic and call upon their spells using forbidden words of power gained from dark entities.

Soulbond: A Magical binding between two people who are destined to be together for the rest of their lives. Rare among the races and extremely rare to cross race. Dwarves call it Heartbonded.
Syn'ella: Faerie and Warrior of the Ninth Thorn from Tsir'illia. She is only two feet tall with gossamer wings, long golden hair, and golden eyes. Soulbonded to Alant Landsir
The Code of the Knights: This huge book is located in the capital city of Branth. It's thousands of pages detailing everything a Knight of the Realm would need to act with both honor and courage in everyday life, hopefully, to aspire to Lord Knight someday.
Tolandra Asil: Half-faerie Queen of Tsir'illia. She lives in the isolated Queen's Tower in the north of Tsir'illia. Tolandra has long white hair, large gossamer wings, and deep sapphire eyes, and is a mix of elven and faerie descent.
Tsir'illia: Nation of elves and faeries in the north of Alian'tir. Ruled by an elected Queen or King and protected by elven wizards. It rests in the Forest of Tsir and all but its capital—Dyln'ir—is hidden from view.
Wizard: All wizards are either elven or half-elven and are trained in Tsir'illia. Wizards use hand gestures to command magic with grace and skill, and need no stones or words of power.
Xarvan Tor: Subterranean city of the dwarves in Lorant. Home to the dwarven war guild, this fortified city lies deep under the Starsky Mountains.
Xil Iliad: Half-dark elf and prophetic wizard. He lives on the Isle of Raer'drin in Castle Wrath. He has faded white hair and ice-blue eyes and has an identical twin, Ril.
Zomnus: God of luck and fate. He is worshiped by almost everyone in Alian'tir in one way or another. He is often called upon before any big decision is made.

ABOUT THE AUTHOR

Born in the usual way, author **Michael D. Nadeau** found fantasy at the age of eight with Dungeons & Dragons. He loved being different people as well as casting magic. By High school he discovered his love for reading thanks to a teacher. She fed his thirst for books by bringing her own collections from home and lending them to him, even buying one towards the end of her class. He has now read hundreds of fantasy books, living in each of their worlds along with the characters. After a while, he started creating his own worlds for his games with friends. Cities, gods, ancient and terrible beings, and histories...then he would burn them all down.

He is the author of the Lythinall series: *The Darkness Returns* Book 1, *The Darkness Within* Book 2, *The Darkness Falls* Book 3, *Dragon Caller; Rise of the Archmage* book1, *Dragon Master; Rise of the Archmage* Book 2, *Tales from Lythinall*—an anthology, *The Curse of Seltemver: Tales of Lythinall* Book 2, and *Angels Among Us.* He also has several stories in Eerie River Publishing anthologies, as well as a few others.

For more of Daniel Eskridge's artwork, visit his website at:

https://daniel-eskridge.pixels.com/

www.ingramcontent.com/pod-product-compliance
Lightning Source LLC
Chambersburg PA
CBHW070225040826
49266CB00032B/476
* 9 7 8 1 9 6 0 6 5 4 0 4 5 *